Marvin Dixon's debut novel, *Settlement*, was published in 2019 inspired by his experiences in the world of financial services. *Payback* continues the story of Justin Kell as he continues his quest for justice. Now retired and living in West Yorkshire, Marvin continues to pursue his passion: writing.

Marvin Dixon

PAYBACK

AUSTIN MACAULEY PUBLISHERS™
LONDON • CAMBRIDGE • NEW YORK • SHARJAH

Copyright © Marvin Dixon (2021)

The right of Marvin Dixon to be identified as the author of this work has been asserted by the author in accordance with section 77 and 78 of the Copyright, Designs and Patents Act 1988.

All rights reserved. No part of this publication may be reproduced, stored in a retrieval system, or transmitted in any form or by any means, electronic, mechanical, photocopying, recording, or otherwise, without the prior permission of the publishers.

Any person who commits any unauthorised act in relation to this publication may be liable to criminal prosecution and civil claims for damages.

This is a work of fiction. Names, characters, businesses, places, events, locales, and incidents are either the products of the author's imagination or used in a fictitious manner. Any resemblance to actual persons, living or dead, or actual events is purely coincidental.

A CIP catalogue record for this title is available from the British Library.

ISBN 9781528994361 (Paperback)
ISBN 9781528994378 (ePub e-book)

www.austinmacauley.com

First Published (2021)
Austin Macauley Publishers Ltd
25 Canada Square
Canary Wharf
London
E14 5LQ

Thanks to all the team that helped with bringing *Payback* to life, particularly Ange, Bill and John, whose support and input throughout was invaluable.

Prologue

The seven old men sat around the oval table idly discussing the politics of the world as they always did before the formal proceedings began. It was fair to describe them as old as the youngest was seventy-four and the oldest would turn ninety later that month.

When they first started meeting in 1979, they were thirteen in total. Young idealists fighting for the freedom of their country, who saw and seized the opportunities to make a profit from the Lebanese civil war and establish a base that would see them control organised crime over the next forty years. They had formed a collective that was so powerful that even the Russians left them alone.

Initially, they did not have a name. There was no need for one. Each of the thirteen controlled either a specific geographical area or had a speciality in a particular field. As the war drew to a close, their allegiance to the old traditions became their heartbeat and the standards by which they operated. They became known as the "Qadim". They ruled organised crime with an iron fist. Their network had cells throughout Europe and Asia even stretching as far as Australia. It was a badge of honour to be a member of the Qadim provided you followed a code that the now old men believed gave them a moral justification for the atrocities they had orchestrated. Children should never be harmed; indeed they had to be protected at all costs. The women enslaved in prostitution should be treated with respect. Wherever possible, killing on holy days must be avoided; and so on.

The governing body of the now seven old men is called the Maktab. They set these rules and expect them to be followed. But as their numbers slowly dwindled over the years so did the respect of the new generation for the old traditions. New groups were being established that operated without restraint. They were small and opportunistic but their influence was growing. As had happened in 1979, one group saw the prospect to challenge what had gone before by bringing together and disciplining these disparate factions to create a cohesive organisation capable of bringing down the Qadim. They called themselves the Aljadid and they were one of the two items on the agenda of the Maktab's meeting. The other was Alfio Mignemi.

They did not have an appointed leader but they deferred to the elder statesman to control their meetings.

'Let us begin.' The room went quiet and they turned to face their oldest member. As usual, the talking was direct and to the point.

'We are old and the fight we face with the Aljadid is one that may be beyond our control. We need new blood at this table. New energy, new ideas, and new steel. We could all die tomorrow and then what would happen?'

It was the youngest who answered what was supposed to be a rhetorical question.

'The Aljadid scum would take over. It would be fast and brutal. The Qadim would be no more.'

'You are correct, my friend. That is why we must change our tradition and bring youth into our midst. We must start rebuilding from within and we must do it now to give us time to pass on our wisdom.'

He paused and looked at his six comrades to see if there was any dissension. There was not.

'Then I propose we invite our Brother Alfio Mignemi to take a seat at this table and give him the authority to appoint others to join him.'

'But what about the problems in London? He must surely be held accountable for the premature end of the Horizon operation?' this time it was the second in the loose hierarchy who spoke.

'We will use Alfio to kill two birds with one stone. He will be set the task of destroying the Aljadid, freeing our foot soldiers in London and his prize will be a seat at this table. Does anyone have any objections?'

One by one, they shook their heads and muttered their approval of the plan.

Again it was the youngest who asked the obvious question.

'What if he fails? He is just one man against an army.'

'If he fails then it is likely we are all doomed. Our network is crumbling from within. The Aljadid will be dominant and we will be history.'

This time it was the number four who spoke. 'I know Alfio; he'll feel that he is being punished by giving him such a task. He knows no one has ever been asked to join our inner sanctum. He will probably feel that this is just our way to get rid of him. Is this the way we should treat a loyal soldier?'

The oldest sighed and shook his head. 'We all know the loyalty that Alfio has shown. The fact that the London operation did not work out as we expected is a wound he needs to tend. This way, he can cleanse his soul and reap the greatest reward. Trust me, please. This is the only way.'

As no one had anything further to say, the meeting was over and the dice had been rolled.

Chapter 1

Every morning as wakefulness slowly crept into his senses from the darkness of the previous night's sleep, his first conscious act was to listen to the sounds of the new day. The rumble of the underground, cars slowly grinding their way down the A12, bins being collected, deliveries being made. These were the sounds that gave Jimmy Skaa the comfort of knowing he was "out" and today was the day when his new life would begin, his luck would change, and his miserable existence might just start to get a little better.

When he was satisfied that his release from The Scrubs had not been a bizarre trick of his addled mind, he pulled back the thin duvet, got out of the camp bed, and walked the three steps to the curtain that sectioned off the toilet and sink in the bedsit. There was seldom any hot water. Each morning he had the most basic of washes, did what he could with his electric razor, and selected which of his two pairs of jeans and two sweatshirts was going to see him through the day.

The fridge that sat under the window had not worked since he'd "moved in" three weeks ago. He kept a carton of milk on the windowsill and a small box of tea bags in the cupboard next to the two-ringed gas hob. He checked the milk to make sure it hadn't gone off, filled the kettle, and sat back on the bed waiting for the water to boil.

He didn't consciously try to think of anything as he sat staring at the kettle. His mind now operated on autopilot, always reliving the worst and most horrific moments from the seven years he spent inside. He'd known that being a convicted copper would make life hard for him in prison. Despite the fact he'd had assurances from the authorities that they would do their best to keep his former profession secret from the other inmates, it didn't take long for it to become common knowledge that he'd been put away for his involvement in a people trafficking ring.

What made it worse was women and children were involved and the case had made national news as the Chief Constable of Kent police had been the ringleader. It all added up to a violent and abusive seven-year stint, which for the most part, the screws turned a blind eye to the regular beatings he was subjected to. The most horrific happened just six months into his stretch. At the time he was still sharing a cell. Gary Jones had made it clear—as soon as he found out that he was a copper—that it was his sole purpose in life to ensure the police scum would only be leaving prison in a box. The beatings always happened in their cell when, conveniently, the guards were on the other side of the landing and didn't have their hearing aids turned up high enough to hear his screams. It was always Jones plus two. The first couple of times they left his face alone. They'd take it in turns of two holding him down while the third punched and kicked him all over his body. The first time, they just left some serious bruising and no one was any wiser. The second beating was so intense; they left him coughing up blood and lying on the cell floor with every movement he tried to make pure agony. He spent a week in the infirmary and when he came back to his cell, Jones calmly informed him that the next beating would kill him.

From that point the waiting, panicked anticipation, and stress of wondering when the attack would happen almost tipped him over the edge. He delayed returning to his cell until the last possible moment and stuck as close to the guards whenever he could. Sleep was virtually impossible and after a month of waiting for the inevitable, he started planning his own death. Afterwards, when he looked back he was surprised that he hadn't thought of suicide earlier.

It happened on a Sunday morning. The cell doors slid open and the guards counted everyone out as they headed for the showers and breakfast. This morning, Jonesy just stood in the doorway, arms folded and smiling. There was no call from the guards, it was usually Stannich or Bolger who were on their quarter of the landing for the prisoners in cell 307C to get their arses moving down to breakfast.

The kettle had finally started to boil but he remained motionless sitting on the bed as it whistled its urgent cry that its contents were ready to be put to use. He just stared into nothingness as he recalled Jonesy standing on one side to let Billy Craddock and Matt Gilbert into the cell. Despite the chaotic noise of prison life beyond the cell door, he remembered how quiet it was when Craddock slowly walked across to his bunk pulling a Stanley knife out from inside his shirt. It was then that he shrieked. Yelling for help, for someone to come and save him, crying like a little girl. Craddock punched him hard in the temple and then a gag was stuffed into his mouth.

He remembered Craddock's face right up next to his own, the stench of his foul body odour, and the stagnant breath as he whispered: 'Don't worry police scum; I'm not going to kill you. I'm just going to cut one of your eyes out and if we have enough time maybe one of your balls as well.'

The first cut went from the corner of his left eye down his cheek to the top of his lip. 'Just testing to see how sharp this little beauty is.' Craddock breathed into his ear. Just as he was slowly moving the blade towards the eye, all hell broke loose as two screws rushed into the cell. Craddock moved to stab the blade home but an instinctive twist of his head meant the knife just re-entered the cut at the corner of his eye.

The screeching of the kettle finally broke his reverie. He got up off the bed, took it off the heat, and poured the boiling water into his cup.

He reached up and ran his middle finger down the scar on the left side of his face. Even after seven years, the hideous look it gave him hadn't improved much at all. He didn't mind though, it simply reminded him of what he needed to do. In fact, he liked the damage so much that he had changed his name. Not officially, not yet anyway. James Quentin Dodds, former sergeant in the Kent Police, was now known as Jimmy Skaa.

He thought the name was amusing, believing that people would associate it with his disfigurement. It also held a certain menace which would come in useful for what he'd planned. While he couldn't do anything about his looks, he did need to do something about his physique. At a shade under six feet, he was tall enough to try to be imposing, but his time inside had seen his muscle definition fall away to the point where he regarded himself as scrawny and induced a now natural stoop. He kept his thick black hair cropped with a buzz cut that hid the emerging grey but his eyes retained their sharp crystal blue.

He finished his tea, grabbed his parka from the back of the door, and set off to Leytonstone tube station to start putting his master plan into action.

Elaine, his wife of now ten years, hadn't exactly left him as she understood what side her bread was buttered, but there was no desire on either part for them to return to being a couple. For a modest share of the proceeds from his extra-curricular activities, they'd agreed prior to the trial that she would safeguard his stash which was a mixture of cash and false bank accounts. For this, she could move on with her life with no strings attached. She still lived in their house in Hempstead just outside Gillingham where he'd arranged to meet her together with a contact who had sorted out his new identity and legit bank accounts.

By the time he got the Central Line to Bank, walked down to Cannon Street, and got the train out to Kent, it was gone 11:00 am when he knocked on the door of a modern end of terrace house in Lamplighters Road. Elaine answered the door and he stepped straight into the tidy lounge which doubled as the dining room. There was a guy sitting at the table, Frankie Malone, a career criminal who Jimmy had first come across during his time on the force. Frankie was the "go-to" guy for any type of forgery from passports and driving licences to cash and paintings. He'd done several stints inside and the fact that he was now pushing seventy hadn't changed his work ethic.

'Good to see you again, Frankie.' The men shook hands and Jimmy gave his wife a peck on the cheek.

'I've got everything you asked for Jimmy, but I must say that name made me smile. Skaa, what's all that about?'

'I chose it because it made me smile as well. Let's just say it's a play on words. Now, have you sorted the bank account out?'

'Everything is as you requested. There's five grand in cash with the remaining £60k in accounts with Barclays. The current account is loaded with £10k with the balance in a reserve account earning a pittance of interest. You can manage it online so you don't have to go into any branches. It's registered to this address but no paper statements will be sent. Elaine has received her cut and I've been paid too. Here's your driving license but no passport as you requested. I can sort that later if needed.'

Jimmy took a while to take it all in. A new identity, cash in the bank, and most importantly a purpose that was back in his life.

'Thanks, Frankie; I appreciate what you've done here. Come on Elaine, get the kettle on; I'm parched and I wouldn't mind a bit of bacon and eggs, I'm starving too!'

While Jimmy tucked into his bacon and eggs, Frankie talked about the scams and jobs he was currently involved with. How the Russians were taking over organised crime in the capital and how there were still a number of good capable small crews, particularly in the East End who would welcome Jimmy into their midst.

'Maybe that's one for down the line,' said Jimmy. 'I've got my own plans in the short term, some stuff I need to take care of.' When he didn't continue, Frankie asked the obvious question.

'What's that then, you got some big job planned? I have contacts that can help with anything. You know that, don't you?'

'Thanks, Frankie, but these are jobs that I need to do on my own. It involves taking care of a few people who didn't treat me with the respect I deserved during my time inside.'

'Who's that then?' asked Frankie.

'A bent screw, a former cellmate, and the twat that gave me this,' replied Frankie pointing at his scar. 'There was another screw scumbag, Bolger, but he went and died of cancer last year, which hopefully was a long and lingering death 'cos that's what the others are going to get.'

'You sure you can do this on your own?'

'I have to do it on my own, Frankie. Then I can move on.'

Elaine just sat watching the television, hoping that Jimmy would be on way as soon as possible. As he stood to leave, gathering up the paperwork and stuffing the cash into his backpack, she switched over for the BBC News at one o'clock.

The headline story was about the trial of some mafia-type and the murder of a financial guy from the city last year. Jimmy glanced at the screen as he went to leave.

There was a man walking down the steps of the Old Bailey whose face was familiar. After a couple of seconds, the penny dropped.

'Well, well. Justin bloody Kell. That's another name going on the list. I am going to be busy.'

He leaned down, pecked his wife on the cheek, and walked out of his old home for the last time, smiling to himself. 'Who would have thought,' he muttered. 'Justin bloody Kell, you've just made my day.'

Chapter 2

With his new identity and access to funds, Jimmy set about ticking things off his list. Initially, he kept the list in his head as he was paranoid about writing anything down, it being discovered later and taken off him by one of the screws. It was during his recovery from the attack which gave him the inspiration for his change of name, then he started to formulate how he was going to extract his revenge. It was during the six weeks he spent in the prison hospital that the idea of listing everything he needed to do first came to him.

When he returned to the wing, they gave him a single cell for his own safety with the guards keeping a close eye on him. None of his fellow internees made any attempt to befriend him, which suited him just fine. He complied with every request from the screws and spent as much time as he could in his cell. He didn't feel lonely. He just spent hour after hour, day after day thinking about his lists, prioritising what he needed to do and how he would do it.

While his mind remained focussed on his objectives, there were times when he got confused and troubled about what he was planning. This led to him having conversations with himself in an attempt to seek out the flaws in his plans, what the risks were, and the chances of him getting caught. Initially, this helped and the lists he was now happy to commit to paper had more structure and followed a logic that he understood. However, over time these internal dialogues started to change. It was as though he was no longer in control of the other side of his thinking. These thoughts took on a *Voice* that would randomly question his plans, becoming really prominent when he was reviewing and updating the lists. At other times the *Voice* was like a buzzing at the back of his mind, as though it was waiting patiently to be called upon.

Since he got out he hadn't had the need to review his lists but now that he could actually start to tick things off them, he wanted to get back to his bedsit and plan his next steps, particularly now he had an extra name to consider, Justin Kell.

On the train back to London, he shut his eyes and thought back to the trial that had put him away for seven years. His plea that he'd been forced into the operation by the Chief Constable didn't hold much sway with the jury, whereas, the testimony of who would turn out to be Justin Kell, did.

As an undercover officer, Kell gave his testimony from behind a screen in the court, which was somewhat pointless. By the time the case came to trial, Kell had left the police and everyone associated with the case knew he was the undercover cop who helped break the case and came close to being beaten to death in doing so. He remembered how Kell had appeared out of the blue one day and got known as Northy because of his Mancunian accent. It was Skaa himself who had checked out his back story of the offences and prison time he'd done and everything appeared kosher. He got his place on the crew and quickly rose through the hierarchy, eventually taking over from the lunatic Sod who got put away for nearly killing his girlfriend. He got rumbled when the last shipment went wrong and was about to be incinerated when the bloody cavalry arrived.

But Jimmy never forgot a face and this time he was going to make sure that Kell didn't miss his appointment with an extremely hot and painful death.

Back at the bedsit, he got out his black notebook and flicked through his numerous early lists until he came to what he regarded as his "number one list". This was the one that had five names on it:

Jones
Craddock
Gilbert
Stannich
Bolger

Bolger was carefully crossed out having lost his battle with cancer and he briefly thought about the position that Kell would take. The order was determined by how difficult he thought the hit would be. He decided it would be sensible to start easy and leave the most difficult till last. This resulted in his former cellmate Jones being first. He wasn't a particularly big guy like Craddock or a fitness fanatic like Gilbert, so he deduced he would make a relatively easy first target. The prison guard, Stannich, was still working at the Scrubs and would thus be the most difficult, putting him last. But where to place Justin Kell?

He decided it would take him some time to consider and would doubtlessly involve changing the order on numerous occasions, so he turned the page to his "number two list".

This contained all the practical things he needed to do and what better way to make sure you don't miss anything than to make a list? This one ran to over four pages and whenever he decided it needed to be checked it could take days for him to be satisfied that once again, everything was in the right order.

The first two items on "number two list" were *Name*, followed by *Identity*. Initially, he had real trouble deciding if these were one and the same thing. In the end, he realised that he could actually call himself anything he wanted, so *Name* had its own place on the list. Now that he had official confirmation, he got out his black felt tip pen and proudly ticked the first two items off. Third on the list was *Money,* so with a flourish, this was also marked as complete.

He could sense the *Voice* in his head acknowledging the progress but urging him to keep focused and get on with the next task which was finding suitable accommodation for what he had planned.

He stuffed his few items of clothes into his backpack and left the bedsit leaving half a carton of milk on the windowsill. After all, it couldn't be that difficult to find the kind of place he wanted.

However, by the time it got to five o'clock, he realised that renting a flat was not something you could achieve in one afternoon. He had managed to make two appointments for the following day but taking up residence in a ground floor flat with a basement that was currently empty (the specification was on the list) was going to take longer than he thought. So, returning to his bedsit with a McDonalds for sustenance, he planned to spend the evening fine-tuning his thoughts on how he was going to kill Jonesy and just where Justin Kell would slot onto the "number one list".

The first flat he viewed the following day was nowhere near what he was expecting. He was about to kick-off with the agent when the *Voice* told him to calm down and not draw any undue attention to himself. The second however was perfect. It was an end-terrace on the outskirts of town which had been turned into two flats. The ground floor had been empty for three months and had a desperately derelict look about it. It also had a cellar that still held various junk left by the previous occupant. The upstairs flat was also empty which really was the icing on the cake. He agreed to take the ground floor residence then and there and went back to the estate agent's office to complete the paperwork. The agent didn't bother to check the references that Jimmy had been given by Frankie Malone, forged of course. The property was under a compulsory purchase order and would be demolished within twelve months. He advised against spending anything significant on the property in view of the impending demolition and made no comment about obtaining the landlords' consent if there were any changes that Jimmy wanted to make.

All signed, he would move in the next day.

Despite the poor state of repair the flat was in, it only took him a couple of weeks to fit out the place to his liking. The biggest job was clearing out the cellar and making the alterations that would make it secure. The only entrance was from a door off the kitchen/diner which was at the back of the house. It took umpteen trips up and down the ten steps to the area that mirrored the size of the ground floor to remove all of the crap. He hired a skip as he had no means to remove the broken furniture, old kitchen appliances, and the general rubbish that looked like it had taken years to accumulate. He got one of Frankie Malone's contacts to fit a new steel-lined door at the top of the stairs and add some bespoke fittings and furnishing, but otherwise, he just left the space as it was, pleased it would serve his purpose just fine.

During the time he was getting the place to his liking, he did his research on Kell. He was now a freelance journalist. Some of the articles he read online referred to him as an investigative journalist as he played a major role in bringing down an investment fund that made its money out of murdering people. The more he read about Kell the more he realised it would be easy to get access to him and hopefully get his attention for a big story. Once he checked his thinking with the *Voice,* he rewrote the "number one list" confidently putting Kell at number four. At the same time, he ticked off various items on the "number two list", mainly to do with the accommodation and various items he acquired for the tasks that lay ahead. He smiled as he closed his notebook and was delighted when the *Voice* told him it was time to go and pay Gary Jones a visit.

Chapter 3

Amy Speight sat outside court number three at Manchester Crown Court on Minshull Street waiting to be called to give evidence against Darya Llubov. At the same time, Llubov's brother Andrei was being tried at the Old Bailey for the murder of Henry Gray. Both these events were connected through the Horizon Settlement Fund scandal, but the CPS maintained that holding separate trials increased the likelihood of securing convictions.

The third piece of the jigsaw was Alfio Mignemi. He was believed to be the frontman in the UK for Lebanese organised crime who was behind the scam which involved buying life policies from people and then arranging their "accidental deaths" to benefit from the proceeds.

However, Mignemi's trial had been delayed due to concerns over the weight of evidence and the plea hearing had been delayed.

Amy had been through her testimony countless times with the prosecution team and was confident she'd stand up to cross-examination from Llubov's QC. So far, the trial had gone well. The prosecution had convincingly made the case that Llubov had been in possession of a cocktail of drugs that had been added to isotonic drinks she had been supplying to Amy. The effects were a constant headache that developed into a full-blown migraine coupled with chronic dehydration. Llubov was caught red-handed trying to inject a concentrated dose into her, which the forensic scientist had already confirmed would have been fatal, bringing death within 30 minutes.

The usher came out into the waiting area and called her name. Amy followed him into the court, past the public gallery on the left to the witness box that faced the jury who were seated opposite in two banks of six. She glanced to her right and saw Llubov sitting in a locked room with a glass front facing the judge, accompanied by two police officers. The usher swore her in and the Prosecution QC rose and asked her to confirm her name. The questions were straight forward as she recounted how Llubov had befriended her at the gym she attended and how they became training buddies preparing for the Wilmslow half marathon. Llubov introduced her to a new isotonic drink which she'd been drinking for about three weeks before the attempt of her life. Yes, she had started to feel poorly; no, she didn't associate her decline in health with the drink; and no she didn't suspect Llubov at all until the evening she attacked her at the gym.

'How did you become aware that Miss Llubov was trying to kill you?' the QC asked.

'Darya had gone back to the changing room for something and I was alone in the Ladies section of the gym and was feeling terrible. I got my phone out intending to call an ambulance and saw that I had numerous missed calls from my friend Justin Kell. I listened to the message he left and he told me that Darya was going to kill me and I was to go to the local police station immediately.'

'How did he know the defendant's name?' asked the QC.

'He didn't. He referred to her as my friend at the gym. He bumped into her outside my office once when Darya and I were going out on a run.'

The QC asked for the transcript of the voicemail to be entered as evidence.

The QC concluded his questions by confirming that Llubov was attempting to inject Speight with the toxic substance, but due to Amy's resistance it only just scratched her meaning that she didn't suffer any long term damage.

The doctors who treated Amy in the hospital had already confirmed the levels of the drugs in Amy's system and had made a direct correlation to the drinks supplied by Llubov and the contents of the syringe and bottle found at the scene.

'Thank you, Miss Speight, no further questions.'

The defence QC slowly stood, picked up his iPad, and appeared to be scrolling to his list of prepared questions. Finally, he spoke: 'I don't have any questions for this witness, Your Honour.'

The usher escorted a surprised Speight out of the court as the judge announced they would take an early lunch, requesting everyone to be back at two o'clock sharp.

'That didn't take long,' said Kell who was waiting in the foyer outside the court.

'The defence didn't ask me any questions. Nothing at all. Her QC stood up looking like he was revving up to tear into me, but then he just said I don't have any questions and sat right back down.'

The prosecution's Junior Barrister, an earnest professional called Giles Toppi, came out of the court and directed them to the sunken seating area in the middle of the foyer where no one else was sitting. 'What was all that about?' asked Amy.

'Just as you were called to give evidence, we got a note from the Defence team saying that Llubov is prepared to turn Queen's Evidence for the lesser charge of aggravated assault, suggesting we could agree to a suspended sentence as it's a first offence. We're getting in touch with the CPS and the Met to get their view, but the thinking is that this could lead the police to some serious big fish in the Lebanese mafia. This will take some sorting out, so the Judge is likely to adjourn the case for the rest of the week.'

'But that bitch tried to kill me!' Amy almost shouted. 'Don't I get a say in all this?'

'I'm afraid not,' replied the Barrister almost apologetically.

'What about the Mignemi case?' asked Kell. 'The plea hearing is scheduled for next week isn't it?'

Toppi examined his shoes as he replied: 'I understand there are concerns about the strength of the case. If Miss Llubov were to turn Queen's Evidence, then the prospect of bringing down an organised crime gang operating throughout

Europe,' he paused before continuing, 'well, the politicians would be very pleased with themselves.'

Kell stood and started pacing up and down, 'And here's me naively believing that the judiciary was independent of the government. You'll be telling me next that her psycho brother is going to get an OBE for murdering Henry Gray!'

Toppi did not respond to Kell's rant. He just stood up and walked back into the courtroom.

Kell got out his phone and called Detective Inspector Chris Packham. Not only was Packham a long-standing friend from his time on the force, but he had also been directly involved in the Horizon scandal and was the officer who arrested Mignemi.

As soon as the call connected, it was Packham who spoke first: 'You've heard then.'

'Yes, just now from Toppi. How long have you known?' Kell's tone was almost accusatory.

'Calm down Justin, it came up in this morning's briefing. It's only just finished. You're lucky you caught me; I'm just off to meet with the Chief Constable and the NCA and CTU boys. I'll know more later today.'

'National Crime and Counter-Terrorism; sounds a bit mob-handed for something like this?'

'It does indeed, Justin. The rumours are there's something big about to break and these guys will do just about anything to make themselves the golden boys. No doubt, it will turn into a pissing contest and we'll all end up looking stupid, but in the meantime, if they think the Llubov siblings can help, then the justice system has to stand to one side. Look, I'll call you later. In the meantime, find out what you can about the deal they're offering the sister.'

Packham clicked off the call leaving Justin Kell just staring into space.

'Justin, are you alright?' Amy had witnessed these temporary blank outs of Justin's before and knew they normally only lasted a minute or so.

'Yes, I'm fine thanks. Come on, let's get some lunch. Then we need to find out exactly what's going on.'

Kell's phone rang just as they were finishing sandwiches and salad at the Pret on Piccadilly Gardens. It was Toppi.

'Is Amy with you?'

'Yes, we're just heading back to the court. Should be there in five minutes.' replied Kell.

'I've got the final details of the deal that will be offered to the Llubovs. I'll meet you in the foyer.' Toppi ended the call before Kell could ask the obvious question.

'What was that about?' asked Amy.

Kell put his arm around her shoulder as they crossed Portland Street.

'Sounds like they've done a deal with both of the psychopaths, and I'm pretty sure we are not going to like it.'

As soon as they got through security at the Minshull Street courthouse, they saw Toppi talking to a group of barristers. When he saw them approaching, he broke away and gestured for them to follow him down the stairs to the basement where there were various secure meeting rooms where defendants usually met with their counsel.

As they entered the room, there was already a guy standing at the end of the rectangular table. He stood up and let Toppi do the introductions.

'Amy, Justin, this is Mr Smith. He works for the security services.'

There were no handshakes. Smith just nodded and sat down, indicating for them to take the three remaining chairs.

Kell eyed the so-called "Mr Smith" recognising a spook when he saw one. Close cropped hair, non-descript navy suit, not too expensive, not too cheap, and a stare that could freeze your blood. It was clear that Smith was going to say as little as possible as it was Toppi who broke the silence, once he got his papers sorted in front of him.

'Before I continue I want to stress that this discussion is confidential and relates to a matter of national security. As Miss Speight was the victim of the terrible attack, I have been requested to explain why the lesser offence of aggravated assault has been accepted and a suspended sentence agreed to.'

Kell sat shaking his head in disbelief.

Toppi continued. 'Earlier today, the CPS and the Metropolitan Police determined that there is insufficient evidence to prosecute Mignemi with conspiracy to commit the murder of Henry Gray. Despite the fact he was known to both Robert Dulac and Andrei Llubov and was with them on the boat immediately prior to the incidents that led to Gray's death and the shooting of Dulac by CTU officers, there is no evidence that he had any involvement in the murder of Henry Gray. Andrei Llubov maintains it was Dulac who murdered Gray after he himself got cold feet by not carrying out Dulac's instruction.'

This time Kell couldn't contain himself. 'But I heard Llubov clearly say that he'd killed Gray by injecting him with the drugs and was just about to start cutting his fingers off!' He banged the steel table with his fist sending a dull thudding echo around the small room.

'You need to keep calm, Mr Kell. You are only here as a courtesy due to your previous good service with the Met. If you cannot sit here quietly, I will have you removed.' Smith's tone was calm but there was no mistaking the icy steel it held.

Toppi continued but was clearly uncomfortable with the atmosphere in the room.

'So with Andrei Llubov not surprisingly blaming everything on Dulac and consistently stating that Mignemi had not given any instructions regarding the killing of Gray, your testimony, Justin is not sufficient for the case to proceed. The charges have been dropped and Mignemi has been released.'

'No doubt heading straight back to Beirut,' said an exasperated Kell.

'We will follow him wherever he goes, even when he returns to Lebanon which is what we suspect,' said Smith. 'Our intelligence suggests his employers have a major operation planned which will threaten our national security if it succeeds. This is why we need the Llubovs to give us an inside track.'

'Wait a minute, you said Llubovs plural; surely you're not doing a deal with the brother!' Kell shouted, standing up and leaning across the table into Smith's personal space.

'It has already been done,' said Smith without flinching. 'In exchange for information that results in us closing down a major sect in Lebanese organised crime, they will be given new identities and deported from the country. If the information is not forthcoming or is not sufficient for our purposes, then they will simply disappear. We are not stupid, Mr Kell.'

Smith stood up and left the room. The meeting was clearly over.

Chapter 4

'Can you believe the British Security Services could be so stupid?' Miguel Santini smiled as he stirred the two sugar cubes he put into his coffee.

'You've done well, Miguel. Who will be the conduit between Darya and Andrei and the Maktab?'

'We have a contact in the Metropolitan Police's Liaison Service who is multi-lingual, including Polish. Her name is Maja Sech. We will feed all the false information through her. The details we provided to secure the deal went through their solicitor, my colleague Jakub who selected details about the activities of Aljadid. We will make them pay for thinking they can challenge the old ways.'

'The Security Services were wetting themselves with excitement when the Intel checked out. They agreed virtually to all our terms.'

Historically organised crime in Lebanon operated throughout the world from various centres, which whilst autonomous were ultimately answerable to the Maktab in Beirut. In recent years a younger, less traditional operation had been established calling themselves Aljadid—the new. They refused to be dominated by the old traditions and in their drugs, weapons, and people trafficking; they often overlapped the territories controlled by Maktab's cells. It resulted in numerous bloody clashes, as both sides sought to establish their supremacy.

Mignemi smiled: 'So they believe the Llubovs are Aljadid and will keep them safe so long as they feed them everything we know about the traitorous scum. Very clever. But what is to become of me when I get officially released tomorrow?'

'You have served the old ways well, my friend. We will return you to Beirut where you will be briefed on your final operation. Do not worry, the Horizon business is viewed as a success and now the world believes it was down to the Aljadid. You will play a part in their final downfall and then be honoured with a seat on the Maktab.'

'I'm not sure I'm ready to be a bureaucrat, Miguel; the Maktab are a group of old men who sit around drinking French brandy and smoking Cuban cigars all day.'

'Ah, but it remains the seat of power, and the only way you can change it is from being on the inside. Trust me, the world is changing. Not as fast as the Aljadid would like, but it is changing and we must be ready to change with it or die.' Santini stood and embraced his friend. He rang the buzzer and the door of the meeting room was opened by the guard.

Mignemi watched his comrade leave, knowing that he was being played by his own masters. Loyalty and friendship didn't count for anything anymore, even with the Maktab.

Detective Inspector Chris Packham finished reading the briefing notes from the meeting of Operation Roland. The Met would be responsible for the security of the Llubov siblings who would be located in a safe house in Bermondsey. They would both be wearing tags implanted into their arms and his team would track their movements and undertake surveillance of where they went and who they met. Packham sighed as he put the papers down and picked up his mobile. It was nearly eight o'clock in the evening when he rang Kell.

'Hi Justin, what are you up to?'

'Just viewed some potential office space at the bottom of Brick Lane. I'm getting more and more enquiries from people looking for "off the record" investigative work, I need some admin support and potentially a junior investigator for the straightforward stuff.'

'So business is booming then?'

'Let's just say I'm getting busier. I also spend a load of time chasing people for what they owe me! What's on your mind, Chris?'

'Can you meet for a beer or even a quick curry? There's something not right about this Llubov fiasco and I'd be interested in your thoughts,' replied the DI.

'Sure, Amy's out with work tonight so I was planning on grabbing a take away anyway. See you at the curry house at the bottom of Monument Street; I can be there in about fifteen minutes.'

'Perfect, see you shortly.' Packham ended the call, made a half-hearted attempt to tidy his desk before setting off to meet his friend and wondering if he was doing the right thing.

Kell had secured a small table at the back of the restaurant where they could talk without being overheard. Although it was a Wednesday night, the place was just over half full with the usual mix of office workers and tourists.

Kell had ordered a couple of lagers which dutifully arrived as the DI sat down.

'Perfect timing, cheers.' Packham took three big gulps of his beer before putting his glass down.

'You're either very thirsty or you've had an exceptionally bad day,' said Kell taking a modest sip of his drink.

Packham laughed, 'A bit of both actually. Let's order and I'll tell you what's on my mind.'

Ordering did not require any consideration of the menu. They ordered the same things every time; spiced papadums, two portions of shish kebabs, chicken madras for Packham, and lamb rogan josh for Kell. With a supporting cast of pilau rice and naan bread, it was a veritable feast.

Packham waited until they'd polished off the papadums before getting down to business.

'It just doesn't add up. We've been charged with doing the oversight and surveillance of the two psychos. They've been fitted with the latest tracking chips, implanted into their arms, 99 per cent reliability and accuracy, so we know exactly where they are at all times. We also have physical surveillance so we can check out who they meet. All mobile calls made and received from within the safe house are monitored. We've given them a couple of our phones which also have location tracking, so the only potential weakness is if they use another mobile away from the house.'

Kell interjected, 'It sounds very comprehensive.'

'Exactly, it's costing a fortune as well as going against all the principles of our legal system.'

'But haven't they provided detailed Intel that's put the spooks onto some of the big names in their organisation?' asked Kell.

'That's just it. How would a couple of low lives like these two know the names and locations of the people who pull the strings? They're also promising the details of a forthcoming major heist "somewhere in Europe", but how can they get to know this if they don't communicate with anyone?'

'Where's Mignemi?' asked Kell.

'Flew back to Beirut this morning with his scumbag of a solicitor Santini. I doubt we'll see him back in London for the foreseeable.' Packham paused to finish off his remaining kebab. 'I think we're being played. This will all go tits up at some point and I don't want it happening on my watch.'

'So what do you think is actually going on then?' asked Kell. 'There's something you're not telling me.'

'This is all classified information, Justin. I'd be sacked on the spot for having told you what I have already.' He paused as the waiter cleared the table and their main courses arrived.

'It's my belief that there's a bad apple, probably in the Security Service and probably quite high up. A deal like this must have been signed off by the Home Office, which would take some heavyweight persuasion.'

'Or the Intel from the Llubovs' is genuine and there is a real chance it can lead to breaking into a major European organised crime syndicate,' interrupted Kell.

'I don't think so, my friend. I think there is a very dangerous game being played.'

Kell smiled, 'So what is it you want me to do?'

'Am I that obvious?'

'The phrase involving leopards and spots springs to mind,' said Kell.

'The thing is Justin, I can't go digging into all this, as I've got no reason to. It would arouse suspicion and who knows what that might result in. You, on the other hand, well, you are an investigative journalist and this could be the biggest story of your fledgling career.'

Packham pulled some papers from the inside of his jacket and handed them to his friend.

'This is a summary of what the Llubovs have given us so far. I need you to check it out and see what we're missing. I won't be able to give you any help so you'll be on your own. This is important Justin and probably dangerous, so make sure you cover your tracks.'

Kell put the papers straight into his backpack. He knew better than to start reading them there and then.

'Okay, leave it with me. Give me a couple of weeks and I'll see what I can find out. I'll give you a call if I uncover anything any sooner.'

'No, I might be being over cautious but I recommend we don't talk on the phone. Let's meet back here in a fortnight, same time about 8:30 pm and take it from there.'

They finished their meal making small talk and twenty minutes later, Packham paid the bill and they headed off on their separate ways.

As they were leaving the restaurant, they didn't notice the man sitting alone at a table in the corner who had been carefully watching them all evening.

Chapter 5

Gary Jones was a serial offender whose crimes ranged from burglary to GBH and sometimes he excelled himself with a combination of the two. He got out just over a year before Skaa and, like most ex-cons, had returned to his home manor and settled back into the life that had put him away in the first place.

His probation officer had been a minimal help but had found him a job at a builder's merchant in his home district of Streatham where he helped sort the orders, get them loaded onto the wagons, or ready for the customers to come and collect. He worked six days a week from 6:30 am till noon and got £8 hour cash in hand. This suited him just fine as it kept the probation service off his back and gave him plenty of time to spend afternoons in The Swan with Two Necks planning the next job with his nefarious associates.

Frankie Malone had supplied Skaa with the details of where Jones lived, worked, and the pubs he frequented. More importantly, he also knew his associates and the job they were planning—a series of betting shop robberies with the help of a bent area manager.

Skaa knew he couldn't risk meeting Jones in the company of his cronies so he decided to learn his routine and then decide how to best approach him. He needed to get Jones to come over to his new accommodation and that was going to be the most difficult part of his plan.

The first morning he trekked down to Streatham was nearly a complete waste of time. The train and bus timetables were clearly just a work of fiction of a warped mind and he ended up outside of Jones' flat at 7:30, an hour after he left for work. After a serious reprimand from the *Voice*, they agreed he should stay there all morning and check out Jones' afternoon routine. He spent the time getting familiar with the local area, the pubs that Jones was known to frequent, including The Swan with Two Necks and guessing the route he would take when he left work. Following a late morning coffee and bacon sandwich in a greasy spoon close to the builder's merchant, he was fully prepared to track his quarry.

Right on time at exactly 12:01, Skaa recognised the man—he had briefly shared a prison cell with—walk out of the gates of his employer and avidly talking into his mobile phone. He was extremely pleased with himself when Jones took the route he expected straight to The Swan with Two Necks where he stood outside finishing his call. When he went inside a couple of minutes later, Skaa was left wondering what he should do next. Despite what he regarded as having thought this through in the finest of detail, he realised he had the choice of either waiting for Jones to emerge from the pub (which could be in several hours), going back to his flat in Leytonstone or taking a chance and going inside and hoping he wasn't clocked by Jones.

His plan was to intercept Jones as he approached his flat, which was on the third floor of a nearby tower block. Then to convince him that he should listen to what he had to say about a robbery he was planning with an East End crew he was involved with. Frankie had dropped him a few names that Jones should be familiar with, which would hopefully lead him accepting the invite to Skaa's flat to outline the job in more detail. The final step would be to persuade Jones to come over to Leytonstone to meet the rest of the crew and finalise the arrangements for the job.

After much deliberation with himself, he decided to return home where he could recheck his lists and then return tomorrow at just before noon to follow Jones to the pub. He would then be more prepared for the wait so he could follow him to his flat and execute the next stage of his plan. He also needed to bring a couple of key items with him in case Jones decided not to play ball.

The journey back to Leytonstone was much better, taking just over an hour by train and tube. Skaa went into his flat, unlocked the steel door to his recently refurbished basement, and walked down the ten steep steps to what he now called his workroom.

An interior designer would describe it as minimalist and stark. There was one high-backed steel chair secured to the back wall, a small sink and toilet in the corner and two iron rings cemented into the floor. A small table, also made of steel, was in one of the back corners, also bolted to the floor with metal rivets. On it sat a mid-range CD player which was plugged into the only power socket in the room. The player was hard-wired to two speakers on the ceiling; one on the back wall above the table, and the other close to the foot of the stairs. He picked up the two CDs on the table, selected Deep Purple's 'Machine Head', put it into the player and pressed the play button. He got halfway across the room before the music started blaring out the speakers which were turned up to the maximum volume. He walked back up the ten steps, relocked the door, and listened. If he strained his ears hard enough he could just about hear muffled sound breaking through the soundproofing he had installed. Next, he walked out onto the street to the corner of the building again checking if any sound was coming from the basement. Once he was satisfied that there wasn't, he returned inside, went back down to the basement, and switched off the cacophony of noise.

The only other items were steel chains of varying lengths that were padlocked to one of the rings. There was a single electric light bulb that hung just beyond the bottom of the steps and was operated from a switch at the top of the stairs. Skaa had put a lot of thought into where the switch should be located. He initially planned for it to be in the basement itself at the bottom of the stairs, but the *Voice* had advised against this, pointing out the dangers of walking down into a dark room where a dangerous predator was being held captive.

Skaa went through his routine of checking if everything was secure and in order. When he was satisfied, he returned upstairs and started to recheck his lists.

The next morning he set off for Streatham at 10:00, which would give him plenty of time to watch for Jones leaving work. As a precaution, he had a nine-inch kitchen knife in the right-hand pocket of his parka and a can of pepper spray in his left. He didn't think he would need them but the *Voice* had advised on caution.

Right on time Jones came out of the builder's merchant and walked straight to the pub. Skaa watched him from a safe distance. The prospect of being able to tick a number of items off his lists was almost too much for him as he watched and waited for his target to fall into his trap.

Two hours later, Jones came out of the pub with another man and they set off walking in the direction of his flat. Skaa was momentarily at a loss for what to do. His plan did not involve a third party being on the scene. The *Voice,* rather rudely in his opinion, told him to calm down and to follow Jones as planned. If you can't get to speak to him today, then just come back tomorrow.

His fears were quickly allayed when the two men stopped at the corner of Jones' street, had one of those stupid handshakes that everyone was doing nowadays, and went their separate ways.

Jones was clearly heading home, so Skaa now followed him quite openly as he walked up the stairs of his tower block. When he was on the third-floor walkway which overlooked the front of the building, Skaa made his move.

'Jonesy, is that you?'

Jones stopped, quickly turning around eyeballing the stranger.

'Who the fuck are you?'

'Don't you remember, we used to room together at the Scrubs?' Skaa walked closer to make sure Jones could see the damage to his face.

'Well, well, if it isn't the bent copper Jimmy fuckin Dodds, you're either very brave or very stupid coming onto my manor. What are you doing here?' Jones' tone was threatening but Skaa detected a hint of curiosity in it.

'I got out about a month ago, got settled over in the East End, and am looking for someone with your skills to be on the crew for a job we're planning.'

'Not interested, now fuck off before I carve some more beauty spots onto your face, scum!'

'Ten grand for one night's work. We need someone who can blow a safe and add the last bit of muscle we need. I seem to remember that was your forte.'

Jones paused, looking hard at his former cellmate. 'Surely there are guys up east who fit the bill? Why trek all the way over here to offer a job to someone you must hate?'

'This is business Jonesy and while I dislike you intensely, I know I can rely on you to do a good job. I also need to make a positive impression on the crew who naturally have some doubts about my credentials to pull this off.'

'Ten grand eh, let's go back to my boozer and we can discuss it over a drink.'

'I think it best that we are not seen in public together,' replied Skaa. 'I can give you the overview right here and then if you're interested we're meeting at my gaff next Tuesday evening to finalise the plans and start the prep.'

Jones turned and leant over the wall of the walkway; 'Okay, you've got my attention.'

Skaa walked over to where Jones was standing and stood beside him gazing across the suburban landscape. As soon as he put his elbows on the wall, mirroring Jones' posture, Jones grabbed him by the collar of his coat and the belt in his jeans and started to force him over the wall.

'Just remember one thing scum, if you or your crew try and double-cross me, I'll kill you. No mercy, just death.' He let go of Skaa and settled back into his previous posture. 'Now talk.'

Skaa regained his composure before he started to outline the fictitious heist he dreamt up.

'There's a particular booze cruise that runs on the River between Canary Wharf and the Vauxhall Bridge. On Saturdays it does two runs; lunchtime starting at noon until five, then a quick turnaround with the evening party starting at six and finishing at 11:30. The boat's called The River Pearl.' This much was true and easily verifiable by anybody who cared to check.

He went on; 'there is a cash bar on the boat and after the afternoon run, all takings are stored in a safe in a small storage room behind the galley. The average number of punters is between one fifty and two hundred with the afternoon take being about six grand. The take for the evening cruise is usually a bit more—around eight grand. There are six crew members, two of whom work the bar. There are currently five of us and you will make six. Two of us will be on bar duty that night with the other four posing as guests. We plan to make our move late in the evening, but we need to work out precisely the best time. We herd the pissed party goers into the bar area, removes all their jewellery, phones, watches, cash, and any other valuables and empty the till while you are opening the safe for the afternoon's takings. Geringher's got a device that interferes with all mobile signals so no one can dial the plod...'

'Wait a minute, did you say Geringher? Jerry Geringher?'

'Yes, he's sorting out our comms. Mobiles, radios, etc. You heard of him?'

'Who hasn't, he's a fucking legend. How did a shitbag like you get on a job with him?'

'Back in the day, he was looking for some friendly faces in the Met and I was able to oblige. I'm sure he'll tell you all about it on Tuesday.' Skaa hoped he'd dropped the final piece of bait.

'I can sort out a fence for the jewellery and watches if you haven't already got one?' Jones asked speculatively.

Skaa continued ignoring the question. 'We expect about £40k in commodities. These are all bankers and the like who love to show off their Rolex's and Gucci handbags. The detailed planning starts next week at my place. So, are you in or not?'

Jones stood up straight and stretched out his back. 'Sounds right up my street,' he held out his hand which Skaa shook with a knowing smile on his face.

Chapter 6

Jones looked at the piece of paper that Jimmy Dodds had scrawled his address on. 7A Ringmore Street; he told him it wasn't far from the Leytonstone underground, so as he was twenty minutes early he sat sipping a latte in the cafe outside the station.

His sixth sense was telling him that the whole thing did not add up. Dodds had clearly done his homework to find out where he was living and openly admitted to having followed him from work to the Swan and then waited for him to go home. But why would he choose him for what was a straightforward job? He did have a decent reputation as a safe breaker but a crew that's got Jerry Geringher involved, well surely he'd know someone equally proficient? Wouldn't he? Dodds had made the point he needed to show his worth by recruiting the final member of the team. He said, 'it was a test'. Such things did happen from time to time, but it was unusual.

Anyway, now he'd made the journey he would hear what they had to say and make his mind up then. In case there was any trouble, he was carrying an old Colt Cobra, small but very efficient as well as a six-inch flick knife. He checked his watch, the digital display said 7:33; time to go, and check the location out. He was going to be intentionally late just to let them know who they were dealing with.

It took seven minutes to walk to Dodds' flat, which was on the corner of a run-down street with waste ground to the side. He walked to the back of the building where there was the usual alleyway that was the border between the backs of the next block of the miserable houses. The alley was full of bins and rubbish, which the local rat population no doubt found very bijou. He strolled back to the front of the building and checked his watch, 7:47. He could see a light was on in the front downstairs room, but the rest of the building was in darkness. The sound of the traffic on the nearby A12 was the only noise on an otherwise quiet evening. He walked up to the front door and knocked.

Skaa was on edge. The excitement of actually crossing a name off his number one list had put him in a frenzy of activity checking that everything was in place; rechecking his lists over and over again. Now it was ten to eight, was Jonesy even going to turn up!

Then to his great relief, there was a knock on the door. Before he answered he walked over to the cellar door and listened. He bought an audiobook especially for the occasion and the droning tone of the narrator almost made it sound like there were people talking down there. It was a bit clumsy but the best he could do.

Satisfied that everything was in order, he went and opened the front door.

'You decided to turn up then? My friends don't like to be kept waiting.' Skaa was satisfied that his voice sounded steady and appropriate for the occasion.

'I'm here, aren't I?' Jones replied as he walked into the room.

Skaa closed the front door. 'Everyone else is here. They're waiting downstairs in the meeting room,' he gestured towards the door that led down to the cellar.

Jones nodded and crossed the room. As he got to the top of the stairs he stopped, turned around looking quizzically at Dodds. 'That sounds like….'

Before he could finish his sentence, Skaa rushed him like an NFL footballer making a big hit tackle. A startled Jones lost his balance and went tumbling down the hard stone steps desperately trying to protect his head and extracting his Colt at the same time. The momentum of his rush almost had Skaa making the descent in a similar ungainly fashion but he just managed to steady himself on the top step before hurtling after his quarry.

Jones' head hit the stone floor with a sickening thud but he was still desperately trying to remove the gun from his pocket as Skaa reached the bottom and kicked him in his midriff as he sprawled on the floor.

Skaa was on him in a flash, delivering another vicious kick to the stomach. He dropped onto him and sat across his chest pinning his arms with his legs. The gun had fallen onto the floor and lay almost next to Skaa's knee. He stared at it for what seemed like an eternity but was, in fact, just a matter of seconds before he picked it up. He turned it over and over in his hands as if it held some mystical power. His distraction almost proved fatal as Jones pulled his left arm free and slashed at his head with the razor-sharp flick knife. Skaa instinctively swayed away from the sudden movement but not quickly enough to avoid the blade slicing into his right cheek just above the corner of his mouth. He didn't feel any pain but the blood pouring from the gash snapped him out of his reverie and he backhanded the gun onto Jones' head.

Everything had happened so quickly that Skaa was in an adrenaline-fuelled frenzy. He leapt to his feet and pointed the gun at the now unconscious Jones.

'Stop, stop,' screamed the *Voice*. *'You'll ruin everything! Stop for Christ's sake.'*

Skaa lowered the gun and threw it onto the floor by the bottom of the stairs. He felt his face and his fingers were immediately covered in blood. Tending to his own wounds would have to wait. He dragged the comatose body to the side of the room and got to work securing the manacles on the legs and wrists. He attached these together with a small chain that connected specially designed anchor points before threading a larger chain through the smaller one and securing it to one of the steel rings concreted into the floor.

When he was satisfied that there was no way even Houdini could escape, he switched off the CD player which was still droning out its monotonous diatribe, picked it up together with the gun and the knife, and left the cellar not caring if Jones lived or died.

Back upstairs he went into the bathroom and checked the gash on the cheek. It actually wasn't as bad as he first thought and hopefully wouldn't need stitching. He cleaned it up as best he could and pressed a wad of lint against it for the next hour. During that time, he focussed on getting his breathing under control as he replayed the evening's events over and over again in his mind. Eventually, it was the *Voice* who put everything into perspective. '*You've achieved what you set out to achieve. Okay, it didn't quite go to plan, but you can now cross his name off the list.*'

Skaa smiled as he took the swab away from the cut. It had stopped bleeding so he put a broad strip of plaster down the red line and crossed it at right angles with smaller ones to ensure it was secure. He got out his book of lists, turned to the current version of list number one, and with a flourish crossed out the first name. He wondered if life could get any better and at the same time hoping it was just the start of a return of the good times.

Chapter 7

As soon as the plane took off, Mignemi shut his eyes and tried to sleep. Santini had never been one for making small talk and, despite being in Business Class, he had no intention of eating or drinking anything on the flight. He'd manage with the bottle of water he bought at Heathrow. It wasn't that he suspected anyone would try and poison him in such a public space but he wanted to be sharp and alert when they landed as he knew that one way or another he wouldn't be staying in his homeland for very long.

Four and half hours later, the Captain announced they had started their descent into Rafic-Hariri and expected to touch down in twenty-five minutes. Mignemi hadn't managed to sleep much at all, but he kept his eyes closed trying to anticipate what would happen when they landed. He knew he was still useful to the Maktab. Despite the Horizon fiasco that resulted in a key operative being shot by the Counter-Terrorism Unit and the loss of substantial sums of money, he had not erred in his task. Maybe his judgement in recruiting Henry Gray had not been his best, but it was the influence of the journalist Justin Kell that had started the ripples that led to the house of cards tumbling down. He hoped that his masters would see it this way and give him the opportunity to make amends.

As the plane taxied to the gate, Santini turned to him: 'We wait until everyone has disembarked. We will be met at the gate and will be taken to the meeting place. We won't need to bother with passport control.'

Ten minutes later, a smiling stewardess approached them and said: 'All the other passengers are now off the plane, Mr

Santini.' They stood up, took their hand baggage from the overhead locker, and walked to meet their masters.

At the end of the walkway, they were met by two men who nodded to Santini and proceeded to lead them in the opposite direction to the rest of the passengers. After various left and right turns and going up and then down at least three flights of stairs, they started to walk down a long corridor. At the end, there was a door on the right hand side. One of their escorts knocked, opened the door, and stood to one side to let Santini and Mignemi into the room. One of them followed into the room and Mignemi assumed the other would wait outside to make sure they were not disturbed.

Mignemi was surprised to see just one fellow countryman sitting behind a small table that faced the door. He was younger than both of them, maybe early fifties, with short black hair showing a bit of grey at the temples. He wore the standard uniform of a dark navy suit, white shirt, and plain tie. He stood and walked around the table to greet them. 'Miguel, so good to see you again.' They hugged and kissed each other on both cheeks. He turned to Mignemi: 'Alfio we finally meet. I've heard so much about you.' They repeated the embrace and he gestured for them to sit down.

Mignemi noticed he hadn't introduced himself and quickly decided that it was probably a good sign that he wasn't going to die in this small airport meeting room. If he didn't know his name, he couldn't repeat it to anyone.

As soon as they sat down, their host began: 'The Maktab have considered the aftermath of the Horizon operation at length. Not unusually, the views of the degree of success or failure vary significantly. The operation was financially successful, but it was cut short from realising its full potential. In addition, we lost a valuable operative in Dulac and two of our best foot soldiers narrowly avoided imprisonment. Fortunately, with the help of Miguel, we have been able to salvage the situation somewhat and been provided with an opportunity to break the treacherous Aljadid into pieces.'

He paused to stare at Mignemi, clearly with the intention to intimidate him. When Mignemi just smiled back at him, he laughed and continued.

'I see you live up to your reputation, Alfio. I'm glad because you have work to do. We have three simple objectives for you. First, you must gain the trust of our enemy. We have already started to leak information that you have been banished from the Maktab due to the problems in London. You will make it known that you are seeking a safe haven in exchange for information that will damage the Maktab and potentially bring down the whole structure of the Qadim. Once you are established within the executive of the Aljadid, you will be instrumental in their downfall.'

Mignemi said nothing but knew that he would most likely be better off dead.

'Secondly, you will arrange for the freedom of our comrades who are under house arrest in London. They will be the conduit for the inside information you obtain from our enemy. You are aware that we have been feeding the authorities bits and pieces about the activities of the so-called Aljadid, but we need full details of their structure, personnel, and plans if we are to bring them down. You will play the key role in this and success will make you a hero. You will then retire from operational duty and take a seat on the Maktab. Miguel will brief you on your flight back to London, which leaves in forty minutes.'

He stood indicating the meeting was over.

'Just one question,' said Mignemi. 'You said there were three objectives, you have only mentioned two.'

'Ah yes, in my haste I forgot. You must personally kill Justin Kell. Not only was he the key that unlocked the Horizon operation, but he is also seen as responsible for the fallout from everything that has followed. He must die Alfio and you must be the one who kills him.'

They were shown out of the room and instead of turning left to go back the way they had come, they turned right and quickly came to the end of the corridor. Their escort opened a door that was clearly marked as an emergency exit and led them down two flights of metallic stairs. A short walk from the bottom was a Learjet 45. They walked over to the steps where a man dressed in the uniform of a first officer was waiting. He followed them up the steps and shut the door to the cabin. The plane immediately started taxiing to the runway and less than five minutes later was airborne. Mignemi had been back in the land of his birth for less than one hour; he wondered if he would live to return again.

In addition to the pilot and first officer, there was one "attendant" who remained in the cabin with them. He was cut from the same cloth as their host who had briefed them but was twenty years younger. He sat outside the door to the cockpit and made no attempt to engage in conversation. Santini had chosen seats in the middle of the plane, well out of hearing range of their chaperon, although Mignemi doubted it would matter if he overheard what they were saying.

Once the plane had levelled out, the pilot announced that their flight time to London Stanstead would be four hours and thirty-five minutes. It was then that Santini broke the silence. 'There are no slots available at Heathrow so we will land at Stanstead. We have a safe house in the Essex countryside where you will be fully briefed.'

Mignemi just nodded. He had no intention of asking any questions until the solicitor had told him what he was permitted to disclose.

Santini continued: 'The plan is straight forward. We have rented a flat for you in Chiltern Street in the West End of London. You will be supplied with the details of what we know about the Aljadid operation in London. Andrei and Darya have already supplied this information to the security services, which formed the basis of the deal to stop their trials proceeding. Currently, they are delaying providing any more information for the simple reason that they don't have any. You will need to establish contact with our enemy and gain their trust. This should be easy based on the information we have leaked. You fear you will be executed by the Maktab and are desperate to trade all you know for the protection of the

Aljadid. You will be provided with the means to communicate directly with me and I will pass on the details to our contact in the Liaison Service who has access to the Llubovs.'

Santini paused while he sipped his water. 'When we have sufficient details to bring down the Aljadid and are satisfied the British Security Services are about to act, you will free Andrei and Darya. They have tracking chips implanted in their arms. They are like the ones respectable people tag their pets or livestock with, but far more sophisticated. These will need to be extracted before we move them to a safe house. At this point, your first two objectives will be complete.'

Mignemi went to say something but realised the solicitor had not finished.

'You can kill Justin Kell at any time during the operation providing it does not compromise our objectives. Once this is done you will fly back to Beirut as a hero.'

Mignemi just nodded his head. 'I fear the odds are against me, my friend. But I will do my best as always.'

'I know you will. The Security Services will try and follow you. They were on our flight out to Beirut but are currently scratching their heads wondering why you didn't emerge through passport control. However, as soon as your passport is scanned at Stanstead, they will know you are back in the country but we will ensure that we are not followed.'

'Anything else I need to know?' asked Mignemi.

'That's everything I have. You will be told more at the full briefing. For now, I suggest you get some rest. You have a busy time ahead of you my friend.'

Santini reclined his chair, leaned back and shut his eyes. He had said all he was going to say.

Chapter 8

The Learjet was one of the last flights to land at Stanstead that evening. It was late April and there was a distinct chill in the air. The timing had all been a part of the plan. Although Mignemi's passport would identify him as being a person of interest, it would simply raise a flag that he had entered the country. It would not cause him to be delayed at the airport for an interview by the authorities.

The bleary-eyed official scanned the landing card, put the passport in the scanner, and ran through the standard questions. 'I see you're a regular visitor to the UK?'

'Yes, I am often here on business.' Mignemi had been through this particular role play on countless occasions.

'What business are you in?' the official asked trying to sound as conversational as possible.

'Wine. Europe, particularly the UK is a rapidly growing market for us,' replied Mignemi.

The passport and landing card were duly stamped. 'Thank you, Sir. I hope you have a successful visit.'

Santini led them through the airport to the taxi rank where there were half a dozen cars hoping for the final fare of the night.

'You take the first cab and I will follow behind,' Santini gestured to the car at the front of the line while he walked to the one at the very back.

Mignemi's car left with Santini's following a minute later. They kept to the country lanes and there was very little traffic to concern them. When they had passed anything that resembled a junction, Santini's car would stop and wait to see if anything was following. The absence of street lighting made the darkness virtually total. The only sound was the drone of the traffic on the nearby M11.

The cars made several detours to be certain that they had not been followed before turning into a long driveway of a secluded farmhouse a mile outside of the village of Thaxted. They drove round to the back of the building and parked in a large barn. The drivers and their passengers got out with Mignemi following Santini into the farmhouse leaving the drivers to patrol the grounds.

'We will get some sleep and start our work first thing in the morning. We have a small team here who will ensure our comfort. I suggest we start the briefing over breakfast at 6:30. Sami will show you to your room.'

Mignemi stared at Sami for a moment. He was the spitting image of Andrei Llubov, albeit smaller with a more stocky build. Sami took his hand luggage and showed him upstairs to a small en suite bedroom at the front of the building. He left shutting the door without speaking.

He fell back onto the bed realising he was exhausted. He forced himself to get undressed and brush his teeth before getting into the small bed. Less than a minute later he was asleep.

The briefing lasted two full days. The next morning Santini talked through what they knew of the Aljadid presence in London and the details that had been given to the Security Services via the Llubovs. Mignemi was then given a two hundred page folder containing the same information and told he had three hours to become fully conversant with it.

Over a salad lunch, the same process was gone through with the details of Justin Kell. This was shorter than the breakfast briefing and Mignemi found it easier to follow. The dossier on Kell only amounted to fifty pages and when they reconvened later that afternoon, Mignemi felt he knew the man like a brother.

For the rest of the day, they discussed the Llubovs and potential ways to spirit them away from under the noses of police surveillance. He was provided with a small medical kit and the procedure to follow to cut out the implanted chips causing the least possible damage.

'You can continue to read the two dossiers until tomorrow morning. It would be unwise for you to take them with you. We will then spend most of tomorrow questioning you on what you know to ensure you have taken it all in,' said Santini.

Despite the prospect of being tested like a schoolboy on the briefings, Mignemi only scanned through the folders that evening. He spent most of his time thinking about who was most likely to kill him. Would the Aljadid seriously believe he had escaped the clutches of the Maktab who were happy for him to be roaming the streets of London? And if he somehow did manage to convince them that they really needed his help, wouldn't the Maktab simply dispose of him when he was no longer of any value? His prospects were bleak. He definitely needed a plan C and maybe Justin Kell was the man who could help him.

The questioning the next morning was somewhat half-hearted. Nowhere near the interrogation that he had expected. He was in the car by 11:30 am heading back to London to begin the fight for his life.

The driver dropped him on Baker Street, leaving a short walk to the apartment block. He handed him a couple of swipe cards for the building and spoke for the only time on the journey. 'Good luck, comrade.'

The apartment on Chiltern Street was in a new block that had only recently been finished. He was on the top floor with a view of the BT Tower and the surrounding London skyline. Two bedrooms, a spacious living area which included a modern kitchen and a small study provided for the veritable home from home. Although as he inspected his new living quarters, Mignemi wondered if it was worth making him himself comfortable.

His first priority was to make contact with the Aljadid, so he changed into his standard business attire of a three-piece suit, white shirt, and a bland grey tie and headed out for a late lunch.

Chapter 9

Jimmy Skaa opened the door to the cellar, switched the light on, and walked slowly down the ten steps. Jones was lying on the floor, pretty much in exactly the same position as he had been where Skaa had left him the previous evening. As he moved closer, the body of his prisoner stirred and Jones lifted his head. 'You're going to pay for this you freak; you are a dead man walking.'

'Now, now, I don't think you're in any position to start making threats. Sit up and let me have a good look at you and if you behave I might just let you have some breakfast.' Skaa sniggered as if he'd cracked the joke of the year.

When Jones did not move Skaa kicked him in the groin. 'The sooner you learn that I'm in control here, the better for both us. Now sit up!'

Still gasping from the kick, Jones struggled to a sitting position and leaned against the wall staring at his captor. He had a massive bruise on his right check which merged into a black eye and a cut across the bridge of his nose that had dried into congealed blood.

Skaa smiled; 'Excellent, you don't look too bad at all. Now stand up. Let's see if you can reach the toilet.'

Jones pushed himself to his feet by edging his back against the wall. He shuffled using small steps with the restriction of the chains letting him get within a foot of the facilities as Skaa had carefully calculated that they would.

'Oh dear, looks liked I miscalculated. Now you're just going to have to shit yourself.' Skaa howled with laughter. 'Now untie your shoes and take them off.'

Jones had to sit back down and when he leaned forward he could just reach the laces of his working boots. It took him what seemed like an age to untie the laces and then lever each boot off.

Skaa kicked them away. 'Now listen very carefully. This is how your life is going to be until I decide that it's time for you to die. If you behave, I'll release your feet so you can stretch your legs. Just like the exercise yard at the Scrubs.' Jones looked at Skaa's disfigured face and took in the manic paranoia as he raved on and on. He quickly realised that if he was going to get out of this alive he would have to outsmart a raving lunatic.

'The good news is that soon you will have some company. Some of your old friends will be booking in to share this luxurious accommodation with you.'

'Who might that be?'

'Why your old friends Billy Craddock and that psycho Matt Gilbert. It'll just be like old times. But with all the space down here it will be like living in luxury!'

Jones laughed and immediately realised he'd made a mistake when Skaa's boot thumped into his kidneys. Skaa stared down at him as he gasped to get his breath, eyes bulging like a bullfrog.

When he finally had enough breath to speak he muttered: 'They're still inside.'

The *Voice* interjected: '*He's lying. We checked that they got out just after he was released. You've got the details of their addresses in Tottenham and who their Probation Officers are. If he's going to lie to you like this you might as well just kill him now.*'

'They got out just after you. I've checked. Like all you scum they've gone back to their old manor trying to behave like good little girl guides. So don't lie to me!' Skaa screamed.

Jones' voice was barely a whisper. 'They did get out, but last month they did a couple of armed robberies on bookies. They killed a guy. Then the stupid gits got greedy. Got caught when the plod got tipped off on the last job. They're on remand and heading for a life stretch. There's no way anyone can reach them or get them out.'

Skaa stood staring at the broken mess shackled to his cellar floor. He stood there for a full five minutes trying to compute what this meant to his plans and his lists. *'Just keep calm, just keep calm. Let's go and check this out and then decide what to do. You've achieved so much; this might be a minor setback, but we've got all sorts of options.'*

With that, he calmly walked up the steps and out of the cellar. He locked the door and turned the lights off.

It wasn't difficult to confirm that what Jones had said was true. Craddock and Gilbert had only been out for two weeks before they were in the frame for turning over two bookies in North London. On the second job, the manager of the shop did not recover from the beating he took when he wouldn't give them the combination for the safe. For old school criminals, this was a step too far, and they were grassed up by the driver on the job. The police were lying in wait a week later when they went out to do a third job. One of the policemen was still in hospital with a bleed in the brain from the ruckus of the arrest. It was almost certain they were looking at life stretches and there was no way that Jimmy Skaa was going to get anywhere near them.

His head felt like it was splitting in two with the mother of all headaches. He popped two paracetamol and two ibuprofen and collapsed onto the couch. He eventually fell into a dream fuelled sleep where nothing seemed to make sense.

He awoke in the dark with no idea of how long he'd been asleep. He pulled his phone out of his pocket and saw that it was nearly midnight. That meant he'd been asleep for fourteen hours! He was famished and decided that he'd walk up to the high street to get some food. His headache was easing and the anxiety he'd felt following the news about Craddock and Gilbert had fallen away. With some food inside him, he reckoned he'd be able to face his lists and start to make some new plans.

A bucket of fried chicken and a litre of full-fat coke later and he was pouring over his lists, crossing things out, reordering various tasks, and trying to decide his next move. All thoughts of Jones being in his basement had gone out of his head.

It was just starting to get light outside when the *Voice* finally made an appearance. '*You see, I told you it would all become clear. It's obvious, isn't it? Go and get Justin Kell. It'll be a piece of cake compared to that slimeball Jones. He's a reporter and boy have you got a story to tell.*'

He turned to a new page in his notebook and wrote very carefully and neatly on the top line;

LIST NUMBER ONE

1. Jones
2. Kell
3. Stannich
4. Craddock
5. Gilbert

He decided that he might need a lot of time to work out a way to capture Craddock and Gilbert, so he simply moved them lower down the list. Justin Kell was the perfect choice for number two and all he needed was to finalise his plans for adding another guest to his basement abode.

He was so excited that he rushed down to the cellar to give Jones the good news.

Chapter 10

Before he left his new home, Mignemi phoned one of the restaurants that he had been briefed on that was controlled by the Aljadid. It had a Turkish menu and was situated in the backstreets of Soho. He booked a table for 2:30 using his full name. He wanted them to know that he was coming.

The restaurant had no set times for lunch and dinner sittings with the menu consisting of what were described as either small or large plates. As it was a pleasant late spring day, he decided to walk the forty-five minutes he estimated it would take, which would give him time to consider how to approach any contact that was made. He realised this could be taken out of his hands if they decided to adopt an interrogational approach but it paid to be prepared for any eventuality.

He arrived at the imaginatively named *Bistro* at 2:40. As he expected, the restaurant was quiet and he was shown to a table in a secluded alcove which was doubtless requested by adulteress lovers hoping not to be noticed.

A carafe of water and a selection of small pieces of bread arrived as he was perusing the menu. He ordered the braised lamb shoulder with onion bhajis and harissa mayo, which the young waitress confirmed was an excellent choice.

Whilst most people who dine alone tend to have an earnest engagement with their mobile phone in the interludes between courses, he just sat there taking in the surroundings, waiting and wondering if the food or company would arrive first. It turned out to be the food, which was as the waitress advised, truly excellent. The lamb was tender and beautifully spiced with the bhajis providing texture and added flavour. When he'd finished, the waitress cleared the table and asked if he would like to see the dessert menu. He politely declined and asked for the bill.

A middle-aged man whom he had noticed sitting at the bar chatting with staff approached his table. 'I hope you enjoyed your meal Mr Mignemi, and I am pleased to advise there will be no charge. Please, may I join you for a moment, and perhaps we can share a bottle of Chateau Musar from our homeland.'

'Thank you for the lovely meal and yes, I have some time to enjoy a taste of such a fine wine. I'm sorry; I didn't catch your name?'

'Alexander, but I'm known as Alex.'

The same waitress arrived with a bottle of wine and poured two glasses.

Alex raised his glass: 'A toast to our homeland, Salut!'

'Salut,' replied Mignemi and sipped his wine which was as beautifully smooth as it always was.

'Why have you come here today, Mr Mignemi?'

'Please, call me Alfio. I believe you know why I am here Alex. I don't have many friends at the moment and I am hoping to make some new ones.'

The younger man did not respond immediately. He swirled the red wine around and around in his glass before finally taking a sip. 'This wine is like you Alfio. It is a fine vintage. The problem is that when you finish the bottle there is nothing left and I fear that is the same with you. There is nothing left that could be of use to us.'

It was Mignemi's turn to take his time to reply. He didn't need the distraction of his wine he just stared directly at the man who would decide whether he had just eaten his last meal.

When he finally broke the silence, he smiled; 'I am in your hands Alex and you know that I have a wealth of information that will help you and your colleagues. You have one simple decision to make and that is can you trust me? Equally, I need to decide whether to put my trust in your organisation, or would I be better spending the rest of my life living in fear of the whims of a load of old men who hanker after the past.'

'Why have the old men left you free to wander the streets of London? It seems strange that they have just ostracised you knowing you could simply come to us and be of great help in assisting their downfall? I think you might be playing us for fools Alfio.' His tone was calm but Mignemi could see the steel in the man's eyes. It was time to go on the offensive and take his chance that Alex believed him.

'The one thing that separates the Aljadid from the Qadim and its ruling Maktab is honour. For longer than you've been born, we conducted our business with honour and trust. If people did not respect these values we would eradicate them. Yes, we are ruthless but we have pride in our code. You and your kind are mere thugs, relying on threats, violence, and extortion to get what you want. You do not understand honour so you do not understand the Maktab. I have served them for all of my adult life and I have been their faithful servant. The recent problems we had here in London were my responsibility. We lost a good man and two of our foot soldiers are in custody, saying who knows what to the authorities. This disaster is my responsibility and they are making me pay with the humiliation of being cast aside like a spare part. You see Alex, whilst they might be old and foolish, they still have their honour. That is why they don't just kill me. They respect the service I have given them throughout my life.'

Alex interjected; 'Excellent oratory Alfio, but that is exactly what I expected you to say. I still think you are playing us.'

Mignemi laughed; 'You cannot see it, can you? You are so different from the elders that you can't understand that letting me live is a far greater punishment than ending my life. I live in shame for failing them. They've even given me a nice flat on the edge of the West End where they can keep an eye on me. They have taken my passport to keep me in this miserable, dirty city. They are punishing me in the worst way possible. I have no reason in my life.'

He paused to take another sip of his wine.

'So where is your honour, Alfio? Tell me that! If you had any honour you wouldn't be sitting here begging a group of thugs, as you call us, to take you in. You speak in contradictions and that makes me distrust you.'

Mignemi lowered his head and spoke in what was barely a whisper. 'I am desperate and yes, I have lost my honour. They should not have discarded me like a scrap of meat you toss to your dog.'

He was letting the anger well up inside him as he lifted his head and stared at his inquisitor.

'They have shamed me and I don't deserve to be treated like this. I want my revenge and I want them replaced by a new, forward-looking order. I'm not offering you my services unconditionally. I'm offering the Aljadid the chance to change. To become a truly global organisation but one that has honour at its core. You need to separate yourselves from the hundreds of gangs and mafias that fight over the same things day after day—Territory, drugs, prostitution, trafficking. I can help you see the bigger picture and people will both trust and fear you. That is why I'm here my friend. Now, if you'll excuse me I have another appointment I need to get to.'

He got up and walked slowly out of the restaurant.

As soon he was sure Mignemi had gone, the man who called himself Alex got out his mobile and made a call. It was answered immediately with one word: 'Well?'

'I believe he may be worth investing some time in. He has a price for joining us and it is not money.'

'Interesting. I'll trust your judgement comrade. Arrange to bring him here and let's see if you can teach an old dog new tricks.'

Mignemi's next appointment was with the barber he used whenever he was in London. It was also a venue controlled by the Maktab. It was back in the City so he hailed a cab smiling to himself that his first day as a double agent, as he liked to think of himself, couldn't have gone any better.

The barbershop had its "closed" sign in the window but the door was not locked. He walked in and took a seat in one of the four chairs facing the large horizontal mirror attached to the wall at the rear of the shop. Only one other seat was occupied by Santini who sat in the end chair with a barber snipping at the ends of the hair on the back of his head.

'How was your day?' enquired Santini.

'Very pleasant. I enjoyed a late lunch in Soho and got chatting to a gentleman in the restaurant. I use the word "gentleman very" loosely of course.'

'Was he the owner of the establishment?'

'No, far from it. He was just one of the waiters there, although he has certain delusions of grandeur.'

'Do you expect to dine there again?'

'Certainly, the food was excellent. I expect we may have further discussions quite soon on a matter of mutual interest. It's early days and I believe they will need some convincing that my services can help them.'

'Excellent. I'll leave you to your haircut. Thank you, Ivan, a very neat job as usual.'

With that Santini got up and left. Ivan started putting the cape and collar on his only other customer. 'Same as usual, Mr Mignemi?'

'Yes please Ivan, the same as always.'

Chapter 11

Aaron Deeping had a spring in his step. Every morning when he got out of bed he had to pinch himself to check it wasn't all a dream. He'd finally made it! He couldn't believe that after all those years of toil, the disruption that working shifts had had on his family life and listening to the endless stream of customer complaints that he was now a top dog and really starting to enjoy life. And of course, there was the added bonus of Mia!

He'd been in the hotel trade since leaving school at sixteen. Starting at the bottom, as a bell boy, helping guests with their luggage at a mid-range hotel in South London. He worked hard and never took a day off sick. He moved on to help out in the kitchen, waiting tables in the restaurant, and—when he was old enough—working behind the bar. He was a jack of all trades. By the time he was twenty, he was working on reception and although the salary was modest he always had money in his pocket to go out with friends when his shift pattern permitted.

Then he met Brenda. She was a waitress in the restaurant, a couple of years older than him with a pretty face and bubbly personality. They started dating and just six months later, they were engaged. He borrowed the money from his mum for the ring and set about saving so they could get married and find a place of their own.

They rented their first flat in Balham and were committed to moving up the housing ladder as soon as they could afford to.

It was Brenda who encouraged him to start applying for jobs in the up-market West End hotels. She was the driving force, always urging him to better himself. He didn't mind at the time as they were young and in love, but as the years drifted by, it had eventually started to grate.

Roles as a duty manager in various hotels paid reasonably well but it was only when he secured the job at Panache that they'd moved into a four-bedroom semi-detached near Clapham Common.

He got the job as the general manager of the Panache Hotel Group, twelve months ago, based in their flagship hotel just off Trafalgar Square.

The promotion was very timely as the twins were approaching their first birthday and the extra room made life much easier. He didn't resent the fact that Elsie, Brenda's mother, had virtually moved in as she was a big help with the children. He was often relegated to the tiny fourth bedroom which, at least, meant he got some sleep and, of course, he always had the option of staying at the hotel, which he had been doing on a more frequent basis.

As he tied his tie, his mood was dampened slightly by the tightness of his shirt and the fatter cheeks that had started to appear just after the twins were born. It wasn't that he had let himself go. Not at all. It was just that Brenda took no interest in how he looked and apart from work, he didn't go out anywhere. His sessions in the hotel gym had slipped to once a week, and in the last twelve months, he'd hardly been at all.

He smiled as he finished the Windsor knot. His expanding waistline didn't matter anyway, as Mia didn't seem to mind at all.

Mia Beckhert turned up for her interview dressed like she was attending a West End premiere. In her late twenties, she looked every bit the film star. Aaron couldn't understand why she kept moving from various hotel reception jobs when surely she could have easily found herself a mega-rich footballer to look after her. But her references were first class and together with the HR manager, had no hesitation in offering her the job at Trafalgar Square.

His world changed on a Friday afternoon just before Christmas. A knock on his office door revealed a tearful Mia who had just heard that her father had died back home in

Romania. He listened as she told him her life story. How her mother had died when she was two and that her father had brought her up single-handedly and then, somehow, found the money to pay for her to go to college in London when she was eighteen. The story was told between sobs and countless tissues. When he was certain that she had no more tears to shed and it was all talked out, he asked her if she would like to go for a drink at the wine bar around the corner.

The last six months had been a whirlwind. He didn't think he loved Mia, but he did love being with her. Recently they'd been spending more and more time together to the point that she was coming into work on her days off so they could spend an evening or night together.

At first, he was concerned about her expensive tastes as Brenda ensured that any spare money he had was spent on the twins. However, he soon realised that Mia wasn't just a pretty face and was relieved he could turn a blind eye when she crossed the line.

He was confident they could ride out the latest hiatus and then he knew he needed to decide with whom his future truly laid. It was not going to be an easy decision.

Chapter 12

Justin Kell was a busy man. He'd secured the lease on some office space that was above an estate agent's shop at the bottom end of Brick Lane and had spent the weekend with Amy taking deliveries and fitting it out. BT had installed the phone lines and broadband and he'd finished the interviews to find an assistant. He decided to go for someone who he could mould and develop into what he hoped would be a mini version of himself, as opposed to a more experienced investigator who for one reason or another had fallen on hard times.

Molly Cribbs had just finished a Criminology Degree at the City University of West London. She was bright and enthusiastic and came across as more considered than your average twenty-two-year-old. She'd had her gap year when she went off on her own backpacking around South America, and she'd worked as a barmaid and a waitress throughout her studies to get some money behind her. She rented a flat in Kell's old stomping ground of Leytonstone, so she was only a few stops on the Central Line from Liverpool Street. She understood that initially she'd just be answering the phone and doing basic background checks and he'd been impressed with her work ethic and determination to secure the role.

She was waiting for him on the doorstep on Monday morning as he arrived at the office laden with files.

'Morning Molly, can you take hold of these for a minute so I can open up?'

He passed her the files and unlocked the door which was at the side of the estate agent's window. It led onto a small hallway and up a flight of stairs to the first floor. He unlocked another door at the top of the stairs which opened onto a modestly sized office space with two desks, a couple of filing cabinets, and a round table with four chairs around it. There was a sink, fridge, and a kettle in one corner and Amy had bought half a dozen mugs, a tin of Lavetta coffee, a 144 bag box of PG Tips, and various fruit teas.

'First things first. Let's get the kettle on and then we can get started. What would you like, tea or coffee?' asked Kell as he filled the kettle with water.

'Tea please with just a tiny bit of milk.' replied Molly.

When they'd finished their drinks, Kell got down to business. 'Right, we need to get all of these paper files saved electronically. I assume we'll need to scan them, but I want the paper saving as a backup in addition to the online backup. I'm a bit old school and you can't beat having a paper record. A lot of the files are just enquiries that haven't gone anywhere yet. When the records are sorted, start following up on them, and we'll hopefully generate some business. I've got some enquiries to make so I'll be gone for most of the day. Sorry to throw you in at the deep end but I'm sure you'll be fine.'

And with that, he picked up one of the folders and left.

He cut across to Bishopsgate and headed for The Breakfast Club, an all-day eatery where the food was simple but good and sensibly priced for London. The pre-work breakfast grabbers had thinned out, so he had his pick of the tables. He ordered coffee and toast and waited for his guest to arrive. He was concentrating so much on re-reading the dossier Packham had given him that he didn't notice the elderly gentleman with a walking stick approach his table.

'Good morning Justin.'

'And good morning to you, Michel. Thanks so much for coming.' They shook hands and embraced at the same time.

'I could hardly refuse such an intriguing invitation. Very cloak and dagger. Reminded me of the old days.'

'Sorry about that, but this whole thing just doesn't make any sense, and there may be a murky trail to right inside your old department.'

Michel Berger-Smithe was approaching his seventy-fifth birthday. His French socialite mother had married into the lower end of the English aristocracy and he'd been born and educated in the UK going to Eton and Cambridge before entering the Civil Service. He reluctantly retired on his seventieth birthday from a prominent but, secretively, vague position in the Home Office.

Kell had first met him at his psychological evaluation before he started undercover work at the Met. Since then, their paths had crossed regularly and whilst they had never socialised outside of their working environments they regarded their relationship as more personal than just business.

'Would you like a coffee? It's actually pretty decent here.' asked Kell.

'Thank you that would be nice. Black no sugar. So Justin, what have my old colleagues been up to now?'

Kell went back to the very beginning and the death of Mike Jones which was the start of the Horizon Settlement Fund scandal. It took him forty minutes to cover the detail he wanted during which Smithe had gone through two coffees.

'So you believe that the deal that the Police and the CPS made with the Llubovs has some sinister ulterior motive than just trying to crack this organised crime gang from Lebanon?' Smithe asked whimsically.

'Yes, I do. I can't see how they would have information that would lead to their ringmasters. They're just ten a penny thugs who do as they're told.'

'And our old friend Alfio Mignemi is now back in his homeland?'

'So you've come across him before?' Kell asked although it didn't come as a complete surprise.

'Indeed, he was prominent on various watch lists I had an interest in going back as far as the late 90s. He was always the go-between. He never got his hands dirty and never left a trail back to the people at the top. He's such a key player that I doubt you've seen the last of him in relation to this matter.'

Kell smiled ruefully and nodded his head. It seemed obvious when you heard it from someone else and he ticked himself off for not even considering the possibility.

'Have you raised your concerns with the Met?' Smithe asked.

'I have a contact there that came to me. He has the same concerns…'

Smithe finished the sentence for him, '…but can't be seen to be sniffing around if the problem lies with the Security Services.'

'Exactly, or maybe it goes all the way to the Home Office.' said Kell.

Smithe nodded his head as though deep in thought. Eventually, he broke the silence.

'I did follow the Horizon case, particularly with Mignemi's involvement. The man Dulac who got shot by the Police was one of an emerging breed. There is a number of European mafias being taken over by a younger, more modern, and I should say more ruthless elements that have no limits as to how they rule their territories and make their money. Historically, there was an unwritten code of how business was done. A bit like the East End in the 1960s. Territory and operations were respected. Almost a certain honour amongst thieves as the saying goes. There are rumours of rival factions operating from out of Lebanon vying to oust the old guard and then start a war with the Russians and other gangs throughout Europe. It is highly unlikely they'll succeed with the latter but all of the European agencies are concerned it may happen. You'd be surprised how many have productive relationships with the bad guys when it suits them. This could lead one to conclude that your Llubovs are somehow involved in this and thus attracting an unusually high level of interest.'

For one of the very few occasions in his life, Kell was speechless. He stared at the former Home Office minister in disbelief.

'So let me get this right. All across Europe, Interpol and the like cosy up to the organised crime gangs when it suits whatever game they're playing?'

'Precisely. Don't be naïve, Justin. It has been happening forever. Keep your friends close and your enemies even closer. No one wants a change in the status quo and what you are concerned about is likely just one small piece of the jigsaw—the tip of the iceberg.'

'Were you up all night revising your one line repertoire? You sound like a comedian making bad jokes!' Kell smiled as he admonished the older man.

'All I'm suggesting is that this could provide an explanation for your concerns. If you buy me another coffee, which is actually very nice, I might agree to make some enquiries for you.'

'Deal,' replied Kell and their conversation moved on to more mundane matters.

The rather shabbily dressed man sitting on the other side of the restaurant near the bar was watching the conversation avidly. He occasionally broke his vigil to scribble in a black notebook and unlike his quarry, made one cup of tea last for over an hour.

Chapter 13

Smithe finished his coffee and stood to leave. 'I'll be in touch as soon as I have anything concrete that I can give you. You have to realise that my access and sources are somewhat limited but I should be able to get the gist of what's going on.'

Kell handed him a business card: 'This is the first one I've given out. All the numbers are there. You can ring me at any time. I've got a couple of calls I need to make so I'm going to have another coffee and sort the rest of my day out.'

Kell nodded to the waitress and a large mug of coffee got delivered a couple of minutes later. He'd made what he called headline notes when Smithe was talking and he wanted to flesh them out while they were still fresh in his mind. If what he'd been told was true then the fact that the UK Security Services were favouring or even supporting one organised crime gang over another not only made this a huge story but also he realised put him in way out of his depth.

He wasn't seeing Packham until later in the week, so hopefully Smithe would have something more definitive before they met.

He finished tidying up his notes and dialled the office to see how Molly was getting on.

His call was answered on the first ring. 'Justin Kell's office, Molly speaking. How can I help you?'

'Very efficient Molly. Just checking how everything's going?'

'Well, this is the first call I've had. What did you think of my greeting?'

'Very professional. Hits the mark spot on.'

'That's good to know. I've nearly finished making electronic copies of the files and I've filled a couple of the filing cabinets with the paper records. I should have it all finished this afternoon and then I'll start making some calls. I've been prioritising them as I go, so hopefully, I'll have potential business for you to follow up on by tomorrow.'

Kell smiled to himself: 'That's great. Thanks Molly. I've got a lunch meeting at 1:00 so I should be back by 2:30.'

He ended the call and walked over to the bar to pay his bill. A bedraggled looking man with greasy black hair had just paid ahead of him and turned around as he put his change in his wallet and smiled. He smiled back politely noting the poor chap had ugly scars on both sides of his face, one a lot newer than the other. He paid his bill and walked out into what was turning into a lovely early summer's day and decided to walk to Holborn where he was meeting Amy for lunch.

'Just calm down. There's no need for you to go spoiling a good morning's work.'

Skaa knew that the *Voice* was right. He'd been following Kell on and off for a few days now and had all sorts of new lists in his book. The coffee shops he went to; what he ordered when he got there; how many coffees he usually had; what he ate for lunch; which routes he liked to take, especially as he seemed to like walking whenever he could; and to top it all he was certain that he hadn't recognised him when he'd let him see him just now. He knew he looked a lot different from the fresh-faced police officer he'd been all those years ago. After all, he now had a few scars and had let his hair grow a bit. His smug, self-congratulatory feeling was shattered when the *Voice* yelled inside his head:

'What about the plan, you idiot! Now he's seen you, how will it look when you go to him and ask for his help! He'll know there's something strange going on. You've completely blown the number one plan on that list!'

Skaa went numb, fumbled in his pocket for his black notebook, and thumbed through it to find the appropriate list.

The plan at the top, which was the one he was particularly proud of, had him approaching Kell for help in finding his missing friend Gary Jones, who had disappeared off the face of the earth and no one knew where he was. This would result in Kell visiting him at his house and bingo! He'd have another permanent resident in his recently refurbished basement.

'See what I mean. He's going to think it's very strange that someone he just happens to bump into one minute is a potential new client the next!'

'I've already thought of that and it's not going to be a problem,' he said loud enough that people walking by looked at the strange man talking to himself and gave him a slightly wider berth. He was of course lying to the *Voice,* which he realised on some fundamental level meant he was actually lying to himself, but he dismissed this and decided to keep following Kell.

'Sorry I'm late,' said Amy as she sat down at the table Kell had managed to secure in a small Italian restaurant just off Holborn High Street. 'My meeting overran and then I got collared by Mark who wanted to talk about the new marketing strategy.'

'Never mind, you're here now. How long have you got? Have we got time for one course or two?' asked Kell.

'Probably just one. The service is usually pretty good here so we shouldn't be rushed. How did your meeting go with whatshisname?'

'Michel Berger-Smitha,' replied Kell.

'Sounds like aristocracy. Who is he?'

'He's an ex-Home Officer. I first met him when I started to go undercover at the Met and our paths have crossed regularly since. He retired a few years ago but he was able to provide a couple of theories about our psycho friends and Mignemi.'

The waitress came to take their order, so he paused before relating the details of the meeting. When he'd finished, Amy didn't say anything for a couple of minutes as she focussed unenthusiastically on her chicken Caesar salad.

'What's the matter?'

She put her knife and fork down and looked longingly at the love of her life.

'We need to move on from this Justin. Well, what I probably mean is that I need to move on. We can't keep living in the past. It was awful what happened to both of us and we've come out of it stronger with the bonus that we've got a life together. I don't want you or us to get involved in something so dangerous. Can't you just let it go and focus on building up your new business?'

'I'm sorry darling, I didn't realise you felt so strongly about this.' He paused trying to find the right words.

'The thing is it's always been about finding the truth with me. Seeing that justice is done. This time it's personal as well. We both nearly got killed and the people responsible need to be punished by the full force of the law. The fact that at this moment they are sitting in a cushy safe house ordering dial-in pizza makes me feel sick. Add to this that our security services are probably responsible as part of some inter-departmental ego trip just makes me more determined to get to the truth. I'm sorry, but I can't just let it go.'

'Not even for me; for us?' Amy asked, almost pleaded.

'Please Amy, just this last one and then I promise it will be strictly missing persons and catching love cheats.'

'But what about your business? You've just got set up and you need to find some paying clients. This could go on for months and you won't be earning a penny.'

'I've got Molly making calls as we speak. She's chasing up the enquiries that have come in. I'll be able to work other cases alongside getting to the bottom of all this.'

They finished their food in silence and he asked for the bill when the waitress cleared their plates.

Eventually, it was Kell who broke the strained silence: 'As soon as I get whatever Michel can find out, I'll hand it over to the police, directly to Chris, and that will be that.'

'You promise?'

'I promise.'

'Thank you.' She leaned across the table and they kissed to seal the deal.

As they were leaving the restaurant Amy linked his arm and said, 'I almost forgot, the estate agent rang and we've been gazumped on the property in Esher. Someone's offered another twenty grand and there's no way we can compete with that.'

'It was always going to be a bit of a stretch anyway,' replied Kell. 'How about we consider buying a place in the city? An apartment on the river would be cheaper than a semi out in Surrey?'

'Maybe. Let's look into it at the weekend.'

As they went their separate ways, the man with the scarred face decided he'd follow the very attractive lady. After all, a bit of leverage could go a very long way.

Chapter 14

When he arrived back at the office, Kell was amazed by the transformation. The stack of files and papers that he dumped on the meeting table had disappeared and his desk was tidy with a neat pile of telephone message notes in the middle, which detailed the potential clients who wanted him to call to finalise the terms of their investigation.

As he flicked through them, he was aware that Molly was watching to see how he reacted.

'This is fabulous, Molly; how did you get so many to be this interested?'

She beamed as she replied: 'Well you are quite famous you know. I told them that you only had limited scope to take on any more clients. So if they wanted the great Justin Kell to act for them, then they better be quick off the mark. Oh, I didn't actually say the "great" Justin...'

'Wow, there's enough work here to keep us busy for the rest of the year. Are they all happy with the daily rates?'

'Yes, I gave them full details. £900 per day for you plus vat and expenses. And £400 per day for your assistant, again plus vat and expenses. Any work results in a minimum charge of half a day.'

Kell smiled: 'So you decided you're worth £400 per day?'

'Absolutely. It's a simple charging model. This way, the clients are effectively paying my wages and you'll make a profit out of me as well. Simples as the Meerkats say.'

'You lost me with the meerkat reference, but sounds good, very good. I suppose I best start making some calls.'

He spent the rest of the afternoon ringing the potential clients and by 5:30 had secured three signed contracts. The most interesting was with a mid-range hotel chain whose guests were having their rooms broken into in the middle of the night while they were asleep. Wallets, watches, and jewellery amounting to over £30,000 had been stolen in just four weeks. The police had not shown a lot of interest despite the rooms being opened by an electronic master key that all hotel employees have access to. But having done cursory interviews with the staff, they'd put the investigation on the back burner. He would start on this in the morning and let Molly get on with the background work on the other two.

As he locked the office that evening, he cast his mind back to the conversation he'd had with Amy over lunch and wondered if he really could back away from the intrigue and challenge of the Llubov and Mignemi saga. Hotel break-ins and asset location and repossession were the bread and butter of his trade but they lacked the excitement and danger of proper investigative work. Anyway, he had to wait until Smithe got back to him and then see what Packham made of it all.

He arrived at the office the following morning just after eight to find Molly waiting outside. Once he opened up, he handed her the set of three keys.

'Here you go; please can you get another set cut. It'll make everything a lot easier if you're not constantly waiting around for me.'

She smiled: 'Anything you say, Boss. I'll get them done at lunchtime.'

Kell spent the next hour going over his telephone conversation with the general manager of the hotel who was having guest rooms burgled while they were in them. He also researched electronic key cards and their flaws. Practically every hotel and office block in London used them, so there must be some sort of encryption that keeps them secure. Surely?

His meeting was at 10:30 over in the West End; he packed up his papers at 9:45 and headed out to get the tube.

'I'll be back by lunchtime. Are you okay with those background checks?'

'Of course, I'll have them done by the time you're back. Shall I see if I can drum up any more clients?'

Kell laughed: 'Why not, but don't commit us to anything until I get back.'

'Understood, Boss.' she replied giving him a coquettish smile.

Less than five minutes later the phone rang.

'Justin Kell's office, Molly speaking. How can I help you?'

There was the slightest of pauses before the caller spoke.

'Ah Molly, what a nice name. Very nice indeed. My name is James, Molly. Not as nice a name as Molly but it's the one I was given.' The rather strange caller sniggered as if he'd made a joke.

'Now then Molly, does Mr Kell investigate missing persons? I've got a very good friend of mine and he's just vanished into thin air.'

'Yes, finding a missing person is certainly something we can help you with James. Would you like to give me the details and I'll pass them onto Mr Kell?'

'Of course. My friend's name is Mr Gary Jones. He lives in Streatham and was due to come to my flat at the weekend. When he didn't turn up, I tried to ring him but his mobile was dead. Dead as a dodo.' Another snicker. 'I went over to his flat the following day but no one has seen him. I'm very worried.'

Despite some concerns over the rather strange manner of the caller, Molly remained in professional mode and continued.

'This is certainly something we can help you with, James. Now if you could give me your full name and contact details, I'll get Mr Kell to call you this afternoon when he returns to the office.'

'Do you think Mr Kell would visit me at home? It would be much easier to talk to him face to face. I've got some very nice rooms in my flat you know.'

'Erm, I'm sure he will', replied Molly, 'but if you could give me your details, Mr Kell will make the arrangements when he calls you back later.'

The pause on the line was longer this time as though the slightly odd caller was deciding if it was a good idea to divulge his name and address over the phone. Eventually, he said: 'My name is Mr James Skaa, that's spelt S K A A, and my address is flat 7A Ringmore Street, Leytonstone. My mobile number is 07689 311869. Now, I think that's enough for you to know at this time. Please get Mr Kell to call me as soon as possible.'

Molly was relieved when the phone went dead. If all the clients were like the strange Mr Skaa then she wasn't sure she was in the right job.

Skaa ended the call and tried to calm himself down. He looked at the script he'd written and couldn't understand how that bitch of a receptionist had tricked him into giving her his address. His plan was only to share this with Kell at the last minute. That way there wouldn't be any record or note of where he lived. Now that he'd told the bitch Molly, it would be in some file and once Kell went missing they would come looking for him.

'Calm down, calm down. Everything is fine. You would have to have given him the address at some point and if we play our cards correctly then we can make sure there is no trace. Just sit back, relax, and wait for him to call you. Okay?'

'Yes, okay. I understand.'

'Now I think there is a more pressing matter. You need to tidy up the mess that's in the basement and make sure that your guest doesn't die on us.'

Skaa knew that he hadn't thought through the full implications of holding a hostage in his special room. Not allowing him access to the toilet was a big mistake. Jones stank, the room stank, and whilst he wasn't too bothered that rats had somehow found their way in and were enjoying trying to snack on the extremities of Jones' body, he needed to get Jones fully conscious so he could appreciate the genius that was Jimmy Skaa.

Back at his flat, he opened the door to the basement and the complex rancid smell hit him at once. He paused momentarily, wondering if he should go and see if he could buy a gas mask but quickly decided that if he worked quickly it wouldn't be required.

The sight that greeted him as he got to the bottom of the steps delighted him and put concern into his mind at the same time. Jones was sprawled on the floor in a pool of his own urine intermingled with faeces. His smile at the desperate state of his captive turned to worry when there was no movement that acknowledged that he had company.

He walked slowly towards the prostrate figure; 'Jonesy, are you alright, it's me, Jimmy?'

When he got no reply, he walked closer and put his boot under the left shoulder and tried to turn the body onto its back. In a flash that he wasn't expecting, Jones grabbed his ankle and pulled this leg out from under him. Skaa crashed to the floor and a split second later, Jones was on top of him trying to smash the bracelet of his cuffed hands into his captor's head. Skaa instinctively covered his head with his hands and began to try and squirm away from the raged fuelled ghoul that was trying to kill him. The tirade of blows was slowing down; Skaa had taken most of them on his forearms and could sense his opponent was tiring. Inch by inch, he was levering himself across the floor to the safety of the perimeter of the chains reach.

'It can't be far now, push harder, push harder, he's tiring!'

He arched his back and forced his heels to get as much traction on the concrete floor as he could. At the same time he made one mighty effort to move out of range of the assault, the tirade of blows ceased and he instinctively relaxed to catch his breath. That pause almost cost former policeman aka Bent Copper his life, as Jones lunged at him and threw a length of the chain over his head. Whether it was his weakened state or just plain bad luck, the chain hit the top of Skaa's head and knocked him away from what would have been the fatal trajectory. Skaa cursed and crawled slowly to safety.

He leant against the wall getting his breath back, staring as his prisoner-come-assailant. Jones was on his knees with his fists on the floor looking like a small gorilla assessing a predator.

Skaa eventually broke the silence.

'And here was me going to start to be a bit nicer to you. You're not a very nice person, are you Jonesy?'

'Go fuck yourself slimeball. At least I'm not a crazy loon like you.'

'Now now, that's no way to speak to your host, is it? I have decided to let you live a bit longer as I've got another guest who has booked in and we need to get this place tidied up. Despite your nastiness, I'm going to release your hands and give you a bit more freedom so you can make full use of the facilities. Then I'm going to let you have a wash and clean this place up, otherwise, Mr Kell may decide he doesn't want to stay with us.'

Jones collapsed down onto the floor and lay on his back.

'Why don't you just kill me? Please, just kill me!' he begged.

Chapter 15

Mignemi had just finished tidying away his breakfast dishes when the phone on the wall by the door to his apartment rang. It was only connected to the concierge's desk on the ground floor.

'Your car is here for you, Mr Mignemi.'

Despite the fact that he hadn't arranged for a car, he replied: 'I'll be down in five minutes. Thank you Petri.'

With the exception of his shoes and his tie, he was fully dressed and prepared for whatever the day would bring. He'd been expecting a follow up to his discussion in the restaurant the other day but was surprised and amused that they would turn up on his doorstep in what he had no doubt would be some flashy status car. It was so typical of the Aljadid. Always making unnecessary shows of wealth and power. They were like a strutting peacock showing off its feathers.

When he was happy that the knot in his tie was perfectly set and the end just touched the top of his belt, he put on his jacket and went to meet his unexpected visitors.

He came out of the lift, crossed the reception area, wished Petri a good morning, and smiled as he saw that the car was a Bentley. As soon as he exited the building, the driver jumped out and opened the rear door next to the pavement.

'Good morning, Mr Mignemi. I hope you are well.'

'Good morning and thank you. I am very well indeed.'

He got into the car and was greeted again, this time by a smiling Alex.

'I'm glad we caught you. We were hoping that you would be in.'

Mignemi knew that they had been watching him during the two days since his lunch and were therefore assured that he would be at home.

'How very fortuitous. Are you taking me to meet someone of importance?'

The barb clearly struck a nerve. 'Please don't be disrespectful Alfio. We are taking you to meet with one of my colleagues. We would both like to follow up on the discussion you and I had the other day.'

Mignemi smiled: 'Very well. Is it a long journey?'

'Not at all, just the other side of the river. We have some offices in the Shard,' replied Alex.

'Of course, you would.' Mignemi nodded.

The journey was completed in silence. Mignemi had no intention of making polite conversation and his escort was clearly under instructions not to say anything of substance until they were with his colleagues. The London traffic was as torturous as ever but eventually, they reached their destination and walked quickly through the reception area to the lifts. Alex swiped an electronic entry card, stepped into the lift and pressed "64".

They exited onto a corridor of office doors. The younger man led Mignemi down to the end and opened a door marked Wirebound Electronics. Inside was a small reception area with an attractive young lady sitting at a desk wearing a telephone headset and tapping at the keys of an Apple Mac.

'Good morning, Mr Smith'.

'Good morning, Annabel.'

Alex Smith walked across to a door at the right-hand side of the reception desk, knocked but did not wait for a reply before entering. The room was furnished as a cross between an office and a modern living room. There was the standard L shaped desk and separate meeting table, but there was also a comfortable settee flanked by two matching individual chairs surrounding a coffee table. A drinks cabinet was set against a side wall adorned with an array of crystal glasses and bottles of spirits. A man of similar age and looks to Alex got up from behind the desk as they entered. He walked over to Mignemi with a broad smile and instead of the usual handshake, proceeded to hug him and kiss both his cheeks.

'It's such an honour to meet you Mr Mignemi, please take a seat. Can I get you a coffee or perhaps you'd prefer a tea?'

Mignemi took it all in his stride; 'Earl Gray tea would be most acceptable. Thank you...I didn't catch your name?'

'I do apologise. My name is Joseph Callahan. I am a colleague of Alex's with the responsibility of overseeing the operations of Wirebound Electronics. We import and export various commodities.'

'I'm familiar with the business of imports and exports, but I tend to operate at a more strategic level,' replied Mignemi.

Before Callahan could reply, the receptionist brought in a pot of Earl Gray and a cafetière of coffee. Alex had not joined them on the settee and remained standing by the door. The pecking order was clear.

'Allow me,' said Callahan as he poured the tea for his guest and coffee for himself.

They both sipped their drinks and there was an uneasy silence in the room. Callahan finally broke it, putting his cup down and leaning back in his chair.

'The thing is Alfio, we are finding it hard to believe your story. We are aware of the problems you have experienced recently and have no doubt that you were "strategically" involved,' he smiled as if mocking his guest. 'But it is strange that your lords and masters are letting you live freely in London at their expense.'

Mignemi stood up as if to leave: 'Thank you for the tea, but I don't believe it will be possible for us to do business.' He walked to the door but Alex casually moved to stand in front of it.

'Now, now. There's no need to be like that Alfio,' said Callahan. 'Come and sit back down and tell me your tale. And then I'll decide if you can leave.'

The pleasantries were clearly over, so Mignemi sat back down, took a sip of his tea, and began.

'As I explained to your colleague, I was strategically responsible for the Horizon Settlement Fund project.' He emphasised *strategically* and smiled at the man sitting across the table. 'This was a unique and ground-breaking operation. Nothing like it had ever been done before. It should have lasted for years and provided an ideal front for us to launder our money. Whilst I was not involved in the day to day running of the business, I was responsible for its oversight and ensuring everything ran smoothly. Initially, everything went well, but then I made two mistakes. Firstly, I recruited the wrong man to be our fund manager. On the face of it, he was a perfect choice, an ambitious young man with a chip on his shoulder who had literally gotten away with murder. His name was Henry Gray and it was he who proved to be the weak link.

Secondly, I didn't act decisively enough when Justin Kell started to interfere. Eventually, Gray betrayed us and was taken care of. Somehow, the gods transpired against us and Kell lived. You know the rest. The exposure, the court case, the embarrassment to the Maktab, and the wider Qadim network was shameful. It showed the world that we are fallible and it was my fault.'

Callahan interrupted: 'A very nice monologue Alfio, but if you worked for us, we would have simply killed you and your body would have magically disappeared, just like that!' He clicked his fingers as if to emphasise the point.

'I'm sure you would, but that is not always the way of the Maktab. They want to expose my shame. They want me to know that I have let them down. They want me to feel scared for the rest of my days on this earth. Let me assure you that one day in the future, it could be years from now, just as I'm starting to think they've forgotten all about me, the knock on the door won't be a pizza delivery, it will be a man or woman who will blow my head off.'

He paused as if to gather himself before continuing: 'I do not deserve this living hell. The Maktab is a bunch of old fools. They have lost touch with the way the world is changing. They sit back and do nothing as the Qadim network crumbles from within as you and your like slowly take over.

I deserve better, but most importantly Joseph, I want to live without fear!'

Callahan put his cup down and leaned across the table: 'And what is the price for your life, my friend?'

'I will help you bring down the Maktab. Once I cut the head off the body, I will be able to deliver the majority of the Qadim network to you, without a drop of blood being spilt. There are some factions that will put up a fight, but they will be overwhelmed.'

Callahan smiled and was about to speak, but Mignemi continued: 'and I want a seat at the top table. I believe I can assist in making your organisation, how shall I put this? A bit more civilised.'

'How do I know I can trust you?'

Mignemi looked him in the eye: 'You don't. But you have the means to dispose of me at any time that you feel that I'm not delivering. This means that in the short term, I'll actually be looking over both shoulders for the assassin's dagger. So clearly I have the motivation for this to benefit us both.'

'What is the timeline for all this? A week, a month, a year?'

'I can make this happen quickly, let's say in the next three months. Certainly by the end of the year.'

'And how can you be so certain?' asked Callahan who had clearly taken the bait.

'We will blow up the Maktab. I know their routine, where they meet, when they meet, what the security arrangements are. It will be quite straightforward. One big boom and the world will be your oyster. Now if you'll excuse me, I have an appointment with my doctor. I assume the car I came in is available?'

Both men stood up together and Callahan held out his hand which Mignemi shook.

'Of course, the car is available; just tell the driver where you want to go. I'm sure we will be catching up soon Alfio. I hope you have a very pleasant day.'

Alex walked out with him and asked the receptionist to arrange for the car to be brought round and for the driver to take Mr Mignemi wherever he wanted to go. At the lift, they shook hands with a cursory nod and Alex went back to Wirebound Electronics.

Callahan was pacing up and down as Alex returned to the office.

'What do you think?' he asked.

Callahan turned with a cautious frown on his face: 'I think the saying is when something appears too good to be true, it probably is. However, I think we should explore using our friend without him getting too close. You never know, there is always an exception to every rule.'

Thirty minutes later, the chauffeur-driven Bentley pulled up outside a row of smart terraces in Harley Street. Mignemi got out and buzzed the intercom of number 19, which housed various medical professions on its three floors. The driver watched him go in and then got out to check the nameplate. He waited a further ten minutes and then drove off.

Once inside Mignemi, waited in the reception area, until he was called through to the consultant's inner sanctum. He walked in and saw two men sitting by the desk. One was his doctor but it was the other who spoke.

'How did it go my friend, have they taken the bait?' asked Santini.

'Hook, line and sinker,' replied Mignemi. 'Hook line and sinker.'

Chapter 16

Kell got back to the office just after 1:00 with a selection of sandwiches.

'Here you go, take your pick; I got a bit of everything.'

'Thanks, but I brought my own lunch with me. But if you put them in the fridge, we can have them tomorrow. How did your meeting go on the hotel job?'

Kell noticed that Molly wasn't quite her usual vivacious self but decided not to ask any for details.

'It's a strange case. The general manager of the chain doesn't believe that the odds are that it's an inside job. Someone with access to the setting up of the electronic key cards must be sharing them or selling them to the bad guys, but he just won't have any of it. He says he personally recruited all the staff in those positions and has interviewed them himself. Apparently, the police are tending to agree with him, so as such they aren't actively pursuing any lines of enquiry. The hotel's insurance is stalling on paying the claims from the guests and they pushed him into hiring me. It's all very strange.'

'So what's the next step?' asked Molly.

'He's sending over the transcripts of his interviews and the ones the police did, together with an inventory of all the stolen items. If you could start going through them and dig into the flaws in electronic key cards then hopefully we'll start to get some insight. How was everything here? Any calls?'

'Just one,' replied Molly handing him the telephone note. 'It was a very strange call. The guy was weird. He wants you to call him and then go and meet him at his flat in Leytonstone. I didn't like him at all. He was creepy.'

Kell scanned the note: 'I used to rent a flat in Leytonstone, but I'm not familiar with Ringmore Street.'

Molly clicked a few times on her keyboard. 'Here it is. The other side of the tube line from town. It's almost the last street before what looks like some industrial land. I must admit I live in Leytonstone and have never been to that part of town.'

Kell walked around behind Molly and looked at the Google Map on her screen.

'Ah, I know where that is. There are a number of rows of terraces that the council is trying to compulsory purchase. There are plans for a huge retail and leisure park, including housing and hotels. These must be the few remaining houses they're waiting to get their hands on. It's an area that no one goes to unless they have to.'

Kell looked at the note again. 'I'll ring him later, in the meantime, please can you find out what you can about the misper and this Jimmy Skaa.'

Kell went and sat down at his desk, took out his notebook, and started to fill out the full details of his meeting with the general manager of the hotel chain. He'd only just started when his mobile rang.

He answered with his standard, 'Justin Kell.'

'Ah Justin, very prompt, I half expected I'd have to leave a message.'

'Michel, you don't mess about, do you? What have you got for me?'

'Quite a lot actually, but it's not something for over the phone. I suggest we meet as soon as possible, and to save time it would be helpful if your tame policeman could join us.'

'Sounds intriguing. I'm actually seeing him on Thursday night at a curry house on Monument Street. You could join us.'

'Come, come my dear boy. I wouldn't be seen dead in a curry house and also I think we need something a bit more private, out of the public eye so to speak. What about your new office this evening, say 7:30?'

'Is it really that urgent?' asked an increasingly nervous Kell.

'Yes. Make sure your policeman is there and I'll see you at 7:30.'

'That sounded interesting,' said Molly. 'Which case is that?'

'Let's just say it's off the books. Nothing for you to worry about.' Kell got back to his interview notes, making it clear there wasn't going to be any more discussion on the matter.

When Molly left to get the extra set of keys cut for the office, Kell rang Packham's mobile.

Like Smithe, he was surprised when his DI friend answered immediately.

Kell didn't go into any of the usual pleasantries. 'Chris, unfortunately, I can't make our curry date on Thursday, but I am having a selective drinks reception at my new office this evening. It's a 7:30 start and it would be great if you could come.'

Packham immediately knew that his friend didn't want to explain any details in case the call was somehow being monitored. 'Sounds great, I'll have to change a couple of things around but I should be able to make it for 7:30.'

'Great, see you then.'

The remainder of the afternoon was a blur for Kell. He managed to finish the notes of his earlier meeting but his mind kept drifting back to the curious call from Smithe. If something huge was going down he wondered if he could keep his promise to Amy.

Molly's spirits improved throughout the afternoon and she was making good progress on the various background checks that she was working on. When she switched off her laptop at 5:30 and started to pack away her things, she asked Kell.

'Did you ring that weird guy back?'

'Damn, no I didn't. I'll do it first thing in the morning.'

'It's not too late you can ring him now, it's only 5.30?'

'No, it can wait. Anyway, why are so keen that I ring him now?'

'Well, for one, I told him you would and I don't like letting down anyone, even a weirdo. And two, I found out earlier that the only Gary Jones in Streatham—that I can find—recently came out of prison after doing time for armed robbery. In fact, his criminal record is as long as your arm.' Molly sounded really pleased with herself.

'Well, that is interesting. But it will have to wait until tomorrow. I've got a meeting later and I need to try and get my head around what's going on.'

'Okay, good night then. See you tomorrow.'

Jimmy Skaa was just about to ring Kell's office when he saw an attractive young lady come out of the entrance and onto the street.

'I suggest that you follow her. Knowing where she lives may come in handy at some point.'

Skaa was about to argue that his business was with Kell but decided against it. He set off following who he was pretty sure was Molly and decided that the *Voice* was probably right after all.

Skaa could barely contain his excitement when the lovely Molly got off the Central Line at Leytonstone and headed up the High Street. She eventually turned into Browning Road and halfway down opened the door of a ground floor flat.

He immediately got out his notebook and started to make another list.

Smithe and Packham arrived within a couple of minutes of each other and once the introductions were over, Kell made three coffees and they sat down around the meeting table.

Smithe sipped his coffee before beginning.

'This is a very interesting and sensitive matter and before I share with you the information that I have established, I advise you both to consider very carefully whether it is wise to pursue it further. I think the expression is to let sleeping dogs lie.'

'Intriguing,' said Packham.

'I would also ask that you don't interrupt me. We can discuss your questions at the end.'

'Understood,' they said in unison.

'Very well. The relationships between the Home Office and the various factions of the security services have always been fractious. The issues tend to always centre on the scope of operations, where responsibility sits, and who is in charge. It's a very ineffective way to operate when you're dealing with national and international crime. Not only does this lead to things falling between the cracks, but it also allows the less scrupulous departments to pursue their own agendas, some of which can be in their personal rather than national interest. This is exactly what we have in the case of my old acquaintance Alfio Mignemi and the two operatives that are now being monitored by the Metropolitan Police.' He paused and looked at Packham who was listening intently.

'The request to do a deal with the Llubovs came from two different sources. The Secret Intelligence Service, as we all know as MI6, has the remit for foreign intelligence and is primarily tasked with covert overseas collection and analysis of human intelligence with the aim of ensuring national security. And on the other hand, we have MI5, which deals with domestic counterintelligence and security. Add to that the Counter-Terrorism Units, which are a network of eleven regional units and you can see the problem. Both MI6 and MI5 put forward the proposal for the deal but for very different reasons. Could I have a glass of water please Justin? All this talking is making my throat dry up.'

He took a large swig of the glass Kell put in front of him.

'The MI6 view, which I should say I concur with, is that the Horizon Scandal was the work of the Qadim, the old school Lebanese mafia that has semi-autonomous units throughout Europe. Certainly, Mignemi is a known Qadim figure and is close to their ruling body, the Maktab. The considered opinion was, however unlikely as it may appear, that the Llubovs could supply key information to us to gain access to their network and thus bring them down with the help of our European friends of course. MI5's initial position was that they believe the Horizon mess was the responsibility of an emerging Lebanese sect known as Aljadid. The intelligence I've managed to obtain is that this group, which is primarily based here in London, is nothing more than an organised gang of thugs, who are crudely trying to muscle in on the Qadim's operation. Indeed some of the Qadim's networks have started to move over to Aljadid and the Maktab, of course, don't like it.'

Kell couldn't contain himself so he asked: 'Okay, nothing you've said is so outrageous that it surprises me.' He looked at Packham who nodded.

'That is why you should have waited until I'd finished,' replied Smithe.

'The issue has been clouded by Mignemi recently making contact with the Aljadid, which is something no one expected. Also, the coup de grace in this sorry mess is that I have it on reasonably good authority that my old department is actively supporting the Aljadid with an arrangement that would see them take down the Russian and Albanian gangs here in London. So you see, I don't think it's anything you want to get involved with. I've finished so I will now try and answer your questions.'

Neither Kell nor Packham had anything incisive to ask. It sounded like something from a James Bond movie with a plot so complicated that it left the viewer puzzling over who was doing what to whom.

Finally, it was Kell, who brought the evening to a close: 'So if we are to get any further insight into what's going on then the only person we can speak to is Mignemi.'

Smithe's retort was sharp: 'That would be a very bad idea, Justin. Please just leave this alone. Anyway, I have a late supper appointment in the West End, if you'll excuse me.'

He stood and shook their hands and Kell showed him out. When he returned upstairs, Packham had put his coat on and was making to go.

'I think we need to sleep on this Justin. It's way out of our league and right now I think he's right. Maybe we should just not get involved. If you're still free, let's keep our curry date on Thursday and decide then what we want to do.'

'Sounds good,' Kell replied. 'Are you okay to see yourself out; I just need to tidy up a bit?'

'Sure, see you Thursday.' And with that Packham left.

Kell tidied his papers away and washed the coffee mugs, he had just turned off the light when the office phone rang. He looked at his watch and saw it was 8:45. Whoever it was could wait till morning.

As he closed and locked the upstairs door and walked down the stairs, the answer machine kicked in. It was a message from one very unhappy potential client. Very unhappy indeed.

Chapter 17

Skaa's elation at successfully following Molly was quickly dampened when he remembered that Kell hadn't returned his call. By the time he got back to his flat, he was fuming. He paced the living room talking to himself: 'How dare he ignore me? She told me he would ring back, she promised. They're both going to pay for this. I'll kill them both!'

'Calm down now! You're being stupid. You've already got a plan to capture Kell and getting yourself all worked up over nothing isn't going to help anyone.'

Deep down he knew the *Voice* was right. His problem was that he was unable to rationalise his anger. Whether it was because his plans and lists had been going so well up until this point and what was almost an irrelevancy had set him off, or whether he was losing more of his mind to insanity he could not tell.

'I'm going to ring him right now and tell him exactly what I think. He'll rue the day he didn't return Jimmy Skaa's call when he said he would.' He got out his mobile phone and went into his contacts.

'STOP RIGHT NOW, YOU FOOL. If you piss him off there's no way he'll take your case and that means you'll never get him to come here!'

'We'll see about that. He can't just ignore me, I am someone!'

'Are you, are you really someone?'

Skaa sank to his knees and put both hands on his face like a supplicant kneeling in prayer. 'Shut up! Please shut up.'

The *Voice* did not respond. Skaa's mind went quiet. He stood up and called Kell's office.

When he finished the call, he sat down and got out his notebook and started flicking through his lists. When he got to the one he wanted, he smiled and went down to the basement to start the clean-up operation and get the place ready for his next guest.

The fight had gone out of Gary Jones. He sat slumped against the wall, detritus all around him and he looked pleadingly at Skaa as he walked down the steps.

'Right, let's get this place cleaned up, and then I'll get you something to eat.' Skaa smiled as he dumped his tool bag on the floor. 'Now there is just one rule while we do this Gary, and it's important you listen very carefully. If you try and do anything stupid, like attacking me or trying to escape, I will kill you just like that!' He clicked his fingers as if to emphasise the point.

Jones didn't say anything; his dull eyes simply looked at his captor in a dead stare.

Skaa knew there was a certain risk to his plan as it involved him getting within striking range of Jones. He'd considered whether it would be better to sedate him but decided the risk was greater that something might go wrong. He'd discussed it at length with the *Voice* and they'd agreed that providing he was careful then there shouldn't be any problems. The objective was simple. He was going to extend the length of chain that secured Jones' feet so he could reach the toilet and the sink. He also wanted to free his hands so he could clean and feed himself more easily.

He started by securing another length of chain of a slightly smaller gauge to the other iron ring on the floor. This one he'd measured carefully to ensure it was the right length. He threw it across at his prisoner not caring that it thumped into the side of his head.

'Now Gary, I'm going to throw you the key so that you can release your legs from the chain they're attached to. You can then have five minutes or so stretching them out. You will then reattach the securing plate to the new chain and throw the key back over here. If you can do this without any fuss I'll untie your hands. If this goes well, I'll hose you down; give you some clean clothes and a hot meal. How does that sound?'

Jones considered this for a minute which created a long silence with the two of them just staring at each other. He realised that he probably couldn't escape at this point, but these concessions gave him a glimmer of hope for the future. He decided compliance was better than confrontation; 'Thanks Jimmy that would be great.'

The operation went without incident and as soon as Jones was secured to the new and longer chain, Skaa tossed him the key so he could release his hands. He then produced a short length of hose from the tool bag.

'Now take off those filthy rags and let's get you cleaned up.'

Jones dutifully complied. He stood there stark naked and let his maniac captor hose him down in cold water. When this was complete, Skaa went back upstairs, reappearing moments later with two towels and a set of underwear and clothes that he'd bought from the Army and Navy surplus store on the High Street. He carefully put them on a dry patch of the floor and left without saying anything. Five minutes later he brought down a microwaved lasagne and a piece of apple pie.

'Bon appétit, Gary! I hope you don't mind sharing your room here as you're going to be getting some company in the next couple of days.'

Jones just smiled. He knew that this would be his chance to take down the lunatic who was clearly now on the verge of insanity.

Chapter 18

'Surely it couldn't have been that easy?' asked Santini.

Mignemi had recounted the morning's events from the moment he was picked up outside his apartment to being dropped off in Harley Street.

'They clearly have their doubts, especially the one who calls himself Joseph Callahan, but they're tempted by the scale of the prize. If they believe that I can deliver the downfall of the Qadim just like that;' he clicked his fingers to make the point. 'They will go from a gang of street thugs to one of the largest organised crime organisations overnight. The problem they have is that I doubt they have the organisation, personnel, and capacity to bring it all together. If they have the brains to realise this, then I become invaluable to them and, hopefully, they won't have me killed.'

'But you doubt that you have met the people at the top? It will really help us if we can understand who is calling the shots. It's embarrassing we haven't been able to ascertain this through our usual channels.' Santini had stood and was pacing up and down the doctor's surgery.

'If it were me, I'd want to be certain that I was genuinely going to help them before they introduce me to the masters. My view is that this will happen at the last minute at a point when things have almost gone too far for me to double-cross them.' Mignemi showed no signs of the stress he was starting to feel as he watched his friend and colleague pace the room. He continued: 'I expect their next contact will doubtless ask for some information or action as a sign of good faith, so it would be helpful if you could get something appropriate for me to pass on.'

Santini finally sat down; 'Yes, of course. We already have a small number of cells that we are concerned with. I'll send you the details and you can pass these on. They should be able to bring them across quite easily as they are questioning the parameters that we operate under.'

'In what way?' asked Mignemi.

'They do not see any problem with the indiscriminate killing of innocent civilians as acceptable collateral damage as part of an operation. So they would probably fit quite well with Mr Callahan and his friends. Anyway, I think that's enough for today. You are doing well my friend and I'll make sure the elders fully appreciate your efforts. The details of Wirebound Electronics and Joseph Callahan will be passed to the Llubovs. This should confuse the authorities even further, especially if we can make them believe it belongs to us.'

The two men stood and embraced. 'I will be in touch Alfio, but keep me posted if there are any significant developments.'

Kell and Molly stood staring at the answer machine.

'Play it again please Molly.'

Molly pressed the "Repeat Message" button and took a step back as though the machine was about to bite her.

'This is a message for Mr Kell, (slight pause) oh and Molly. This is Mr James Skaa and I am extremely unhappy that you have not rung me back as promised. My friend Gary Jones has gone missing and he could be dead somewhere in a ditch and I need you to find him. (Another longer pause). I've been waiting all day for you to call and I'm very, very ANGRY! YOU CANNOT JUST IGNORE PEOPLE YOU IGNORANT BASTARD. NOW CALL ME BACK AS SOON AS YOU GET THIS MESSAGE OTHERWISE YOU'LL REGRET IT!'

'He's not a happy bunny is he?' said Kell.

'I didn't like him the first time he called. He sounds completely mad. You're not going to take him on as a client, are you?' Molly sounded like she was pleading.

'No, I don't think we will, but I better speak to him and calm him down, otherwise, he sounds like he could do something stupid.'

'Just as long as I don't have to speak to him again. He's creepy.'

'Right, there's no time like the present. What's his number?'

Molly passed him the original note she'd made when Skaa had first made contact.

Kell used the phone on his desk and dialled. At first, he thought it would just go to voicemail, but at that moment it connected.

'Hello, who is this?'

'Mr Skaa, its Justin Kell returning your call. I'm sorry I couldn't get back to you yesterday but something unexpectedly cropped up.' Kell was at his smoothest professional best.

'Oh, I see. Well, at least you've called now.' There was a pause on the line then Skaa said, 'Thank you.'

'That's okay, Mr Skaa, how can I help you?'

Skaa's fury from the previous evening disappeared in an instant. 'Well, it's my friend Gary, Gary Jones. He's disappeared and I need someone to help me find him. I hear that you are very good Mr Kell and I'm hoping you can help.'

Kell scanned the background note that Molly had prepared when searching for Gary Jones's.

'Is it the Gary Jones who lives in Streatham?' asked Kell.

'Yes, yes it is.' Skaa was starting to sound unnecessarily excited.

'Is it the same Gary Jones that was recently released from Wormwood Scrubs, let's see, for armed robbery and GBH?'

'Yes, that's him.'

'Unfortunately, that changes everything Mr Skaa. You see, I don't get involved in work that relates to ex-convicts in any way. I work closely with the Met on occasions and it would be bad for business if I was seen to be helping an ex-con. Apologies, but I'm sure you'll find someone else who can help you.'

Skaa was stunned into silence. Finally, he said: 'So you're not going to come round and take all the details?'

'No, I'm not.'

'But I've got everything prepared. I've cleaned the place up. Everything's ready.'

'I'm sorry Mr Skaa, but I can't help. Now if you'll excuse me, I have a very busy day ahead.'

And with that, he disconnected the call.

Molly heaved a sigh of relief: 'Is it true you won't do any work when an ex-convict is involved?'

'No, not at all. It just came into my mind as I was scanning through your notes. I didn't want to have to say that we thought he was crazy and didn't like the tone of his message. It was bizarre though. I don't think he could believe that I said no. He also said he's cleaned his place up as though I was expected for afternoon tea. Very strange.'

'What should I do if he calls again?' Molly asked anxiously.

'Just repeat the ex-con line. If I'm not here I think there's a way you can transfer the call to my mobile and I'll deal with him.'

'Yes there is, I read it in the instructions the other day,' replied Molly.

'Now, lets' get on with some proper work. What have you got on those hotel robberies?'

Skaa heard the call disconnect and stood in his living room staring at his phone in disbelief. 'He said "no", he turned me down. The bastard turned me down! I don't believe it, the bastard turned me down.'

He started to pace around the room, muttering the same phrase over and over. Eventually, the *Voice* came forward.

'Be quiet and calm down. So he hasn't taken the bait. I'm not surprised considering the message you left him last night. All that crap about not working with ex-cons was just an excuse. You frightened him off, you idiot. Now calm down and let's make a plan.'

Skaa slumped onto the moth-eaten sofa, put his head back and shut his eyes. 'There's no way he's going to come here now. I've ruined everything. All those lists are just useless.'

'You are forgetting something so obvious that it's staring right into that ugly scarred face of yours.'

'What's that then?'

'Why, the lovely Molly of course. She lives just on the other side of town. It should be quite easy to arrange for her to visit, especially if you were to meet her at the tube station. Why, it's only a brisk five-minute walk to here. And once she's signed the guest register, well imagine the fun you could have, not to mention the leverage over Mr Kell.'

His eyes popped open and he sat up with a huge smile on his face.
'Of course, the lovely Molly. She'd make a perfect house guest and who would be the smart one then, Justin bloody Kell!'
He picked up his notebook from the filthy coffee table and started to make yet another list.

Chapter 19

As the day wore on, any lingering thoughts of the strange Jimmy Skaa soon disappeared and it was business as usual in Kell's office.

'There are various suppliers of electronic entry and key card systems, all of whom claim to have the most sophisticated security features. None of them claim to be perfect as they quote figures between 98 and 99 percent reliability, i.e. there's a small chance that they can be compromised.' Molly sounded very pleased with herself.

'I can understand that in office blocks as during the day there are loads of people about and at night most employ security guards and CCTV systems. But it's not a great advert for the hotel industry, is it?' replied Kell.

'Well, you can double lock your door once inside—that's a standard feature pretty much everywhere. Surely everyone must do that when they're going to bed?'

'Apparently not,' said Kell. 'Anyway, I think it's a health and safety feature that you can open the lock from the outside as well. What's strange about these robberies is that the thieves chose to do them in the middle of the night, knowing the guests will be asleep in their rooms. It doesn't make sense.' Kell felt as if he'd completed a lap of the track and was back at the start line not having made any progress.

Molly gave him a quizzical look. 'Haven't you worked that bit out yet? It's obvious, isn't it? They break in then because they know that's when the goodies will be in the room. Think about it. If you're wearing a fancy watch, nice jewellery or have a Mulberry handbag then the odds are that you'll be wearing it or have it with you. When you go to bed, it's the only time the thieves can guarantee that all the expensive stuff will be in the room.'

The penny dropped for Kell: 'Of course! So that means whoever is checking the guests in clocks the Rolex watch and the diamond earrings and passes the information onto the thieves.'

'Or maybe, they do the thieving as well,' added Molly.

'Right, can you cross-check the dates and times of the robberies with the reception staff on duty on the days in question? There may even be a record of who checks which guests in. Good work Molly; you're a natural at this detective work. Now I'm off to meet a pal of mine for a curry. Are you okay to lock everything up?'

'Sure, unless you want me to come with you. I quite like a curry every now and again.' Molly smiled as she spoke and Kell wondered if she was flirting with him.

He laughed nervously before replying: 'Its business and I don't mix business with pleasure. I'll see you in the morning.'

'Goodnight then, have a nice curry.'

Packham was waiting for him at their usual table at the back of the curry house on Monument Street.

Kell looked at his watch as he sat down. 'I'm not late, am I?'

'Not at all. It's me being early for once. The close of play briefing finished on time, mainly because no one asked the usual stupid questions,' replied the DI.

The waiter delivered two pints of lager without being asked and asked if they wanted their usual. They both nodded and declined to look at the menus.

'It's a bit sad really. Ordering the same thing every time we come here,' said Packham taking a long pull on his drink.

'Not really. We know what we like so there's no point risking anything different.'

'Not one for change are you, Justin!' And they both laughed.

'Actually, I might have a bit of a problem at the office.'

'What's that then?' asked Packham.

'My assistant Molly, I think she's flirting with me.'

Packham almost spat out a mouthful of lager. 'But you're old enough to be her father for goodness sake.'

'I'm not that old. I'm only 38 and she's 22, I think,' said Kell.

'Well, I'd nip it the bud if I were you. That sort of thing always ends in tears. Now, I've got a bit of news.'

The papadums arrived right on cue and the policeman put a large dollop of lime pickle on his plate.

'Mignemi is living in a very nice apartment just off Baker Street. It's owned by the Antet Corporation which is a known front of the Qadim here in London. The interesting thing is our friend Alfio was picked up by the Aljadid this morning and taken to an office in the Shard, a firm called Wirebound Electronics. We're still checking this out but I'm certain it will be an Aljadid company. Mignemi was then driven to medical practice in Harley Street in the Aljadid vehicle.'

Kell interrupted: 'Have the Llubovs said anything about this Wirebound Electronics?'

'Not so far,' replied Packham. 'They have requested a meeting with the liaison officer tomorrow, so it'll be interesting to see what they have to say.'

There was a short period of silence while they digested their papadums and what Packham had just relayed. It was Kell who picked up the thread.

'From everything we know about Mignemi, I just don't see him double-crossing the Qadim. If he isn't, then he's playing Aljadid like a double agent. Gaining their confidence, gathering information, and feeding it back to Beirut. He was probably briefed at the airport and then flew straight back to London, which explains why he didn't go through customs.'

'Like you, I don't see him betraying his masters. I think they're using him to get at the Aljadid. Maybe put them in their place or just simply get rid of them. The thing is Justin, it doesn't really help us, does it? I mean, whatever he's doing we can't intervene and remember, unlike the Llubovs, he didn't even go on trial so there's nothing to stop him walking around the streets of London playing James Bond.'

'Hmm, all I really want is justice and that means seeing the psychos and Mignemi behind bars. But with all this going on, I don't see there's anything we can do.' replied Kell.

'I agree Mignemi is the key but it looks like he's being tailed by everyone; the security services, the Aljadid even my guys. So there's no way we can get to him without setting the alarm bells ringing.'

'Maybe, maybe not,' mused Kell. 'Let's keep an open mind on that and see what the Llubovs say next. This will confirm which side Mignemi is on and we can take it from there.'

'Okay, I'll call you from a public phone when I hear anything,' said Packham. 'Now where are those curries, I'm starving.'

At the same time, her boss was tucking into his papadums and lime pickle, Molly was locking the office and heading home for the evening.

She was a bit later than usual as she wanted to finish off her cross-checking of the reception staff at the hotels where the robberies had taken place and she was very pleased that she had. It looked like a slam dunk and she was sure that Justin would be very happy with what she'd done. As she walked to Liverpool Street to get the tube home she wondered if there was any chance he would show his gratitude in a more personal way. She was so wrapped up in her thoughts that she didn't notice the smartly dressed, rather official-looking man who was following her.

The *Voice* had convinced him of two things: firstly that he needed to act quickly and secondly that he must smarten himself up. He was aware he'd let himself go a bit. His normally close-cropped hair had grown to an untidy length and not having washed it for weeks it looked unkempt and greasy. He'd been wearing the same clothes every day and they were dirty and smelled like a tramp's, so when the *Voice* told him the plan he devised to snare Molly, he'd immediately gone and had a shower, changed into his other set of clothes and gone and got his hair cut. His next stop was Top Man on the High Street and he bought a dark navy blue suit, white shirt, plain tie, a pack of three socks, a pair of black shoes, and some underwear. When he got back to the flat it was early afternoon, which gave him plenty of time to have another shower and get ready. When he was all set to go he went down to the cellar to see what his housemate thought of his makeover and make sure everything was ready for his next guest.

Jones only glanced up from his position of leaning against the back wall but managed to say: 'What the fuck have you done to yourself? You look like a right tart.'

'Don't be so bitchy Gary. We've got a visitor this evening and I wanted to look my best.' Skaa did a twirl like a catwalk model.

'Oh aye and whose that then?' enquired Jones.

'It's nobody you know but she'll certainly add a bit of glamour down here,' replied Skaa as he checked the chains on the other side of the room from where his first captive sat.

'That's interesting, a woman is it? Didn't realise you're a pervert as well as a nutcase.'

Skaa spun around and was about to charge across the room and give his captive a beating when the *Voice* shouted.

'Stop! Don't be so stupid. He just wants to get you going and get you close enough so he can knock you unconscious. You've got to calm down if this is going to work. You also might want to think about your clothes as well. Now leave him alone and get into town and watch the office. You don't want that bitch slipping through your fingers at this stage.'

He gave Jones one final look of hatred and stormed back up the steps to the living room. He picked up a couple of items that he'd managed to save before his arrest seven years ago and headed out to intercept the bitch called Molly.

They had a long conversation about the best way to get his prey back to the flat without anyone who witnessed what was happening giving it a second thought. As usual, the *Voice* had been right.

'A simple plan is the best plan. You were a policeman, weren't you? And you still have a couple of your ID cards, so all you have to do is play yourself from your previous life and the plan will run like clockwork. You must follow her on the train otherwise you'll be hanging around the station for ages which will attract attention. So just make sure you get to her office early enough in case she finishes on time.'

When it got to seven o'clock and she hadn't appeared, he started to panic that the bitch must have taken the afternoon off. But just as he was about to give up and head back home, the door opened and there she was locking up.

When the train pulled into Leytonstone, he made sure he was first off and up the stairs and onto the pavement outside. He waited as the steady trickle of humanity trudged their way out of the station and deliberately started to make like he was looking for someone.

As she emerged from the exit she was rummaging in her bag.

'Excuse me Miss, would you be a Molly Cribbs?' At the same time, he flashed his old warrant card and put a serious frown on his face.'

'Er yes, yes I am. What's the matter, have I done something wrong?'

'Not at all. It's Justin Kell he's in a bit of bother and we need you to come to the scene.' Skaa started ushering her down the street in the opposite direction to where the rest of the zombie-like commuters were headed.

Molly was in shock and didn't realise what was going on.

'What's happened?' was all she could manage.

'We believe it's one of Justin's clients who has a beef with him for not taking his case. It's difficult to say at this stage but the guy has got him held up in his flat and is demanding he talks to you as well.'

They were now walking briskly through a run-down area and there was nobody on the streets except them.

'Do you have any idea who this man may be Molly? He's asking for you by name?' Skaa was managing to maintain his old police voice but the excitement and adrenalin pumping through him were making that more and more difficult.

Molly was starting to think a bit more clearly: 'Er yes, there is this one guy, he had a funny name, I think it was Scar or something like that and he was very angry with Justin for not taking his case.'

As soon as she said "scar" she turned to look at the policeman and immediately knew that all this was terribly wrong. She tried to pull her arm free from his grip, but he just squeezed tighter and increased their pace.

'Don't worry, we're nearly there.' Skaa snarled.

Molly swung her free arm which was holding her bag and managed to hit her assailant a glancing blow on the head. In a flash, he stopped and punched her in the side of the head. There was the sound of her nose breaking and she immediately went limp. They had reached the apartment and he opened the door and pushed her inside.

Molly wasn't unconscious but she was dazed. A feeling of pure terror ran through her as he pushed her down some steps into a dark room. When her head hit the stone floor she slipped into the relief of unconsciousness.

Chapter 20

When Kell arrived at the office the following morning, he was surprised that Molly wasn't already there. He wasn't aware of what time she got into work but she was always sitting at her desk when he rocked up at about 8:45.

He didn't give it a second thought until it got to 9:30 and was making himself his second coffee of the day. If she was not coming in for any reason then surely she would have let him know, wouldn't she? They hadn't established any protocols if such an issue were to come up, so maybe she just had a doctor's appointment and would appear later in the morning.

The previous evening at 18:58 she had emailed him the details of her work on the hotel case; dates of the robberies, who was on reception, who had checked in the guests, and a table of the findings which basically solved the case. He telephoned the general manager and arranged to see him later that morning. Before he left, he used his mobile to call Molly to make sure she was alright. It rang out a few times before going to voicemail. He left a message saying that he was just checking if she was okay and to ring him when she got a moment.

He was halfway down Brick Lane when he remembered he hadn't locked the office. He turned back and hoped that if Molly was ill it wasn't anything too serious.

Kell guessed the general manager of the Panache Hotel Group was approaching forty and if he didn't start using the gyms in the business he ran then he would succumb to what everyone referred to as the middle-aged spread. His name was Aaron Deeping and he clearly had some Eastern European blood in his family.

They met in his office in their flagship hotel, The Panache Royal, near Trafalgar Square.

'So Justin, what have you got for me? Have you cracked the case?'

Kell pulled a file out of his backpack and pushed it across the table: 'See for yourself.'

Deeping tentatively opened the file as if he expected it to somehow magically bite him and starting reading the three pages of A4 that were in it.

As he was reading, Kell said: 'I see from the wedding ring that you are married, Aaron.'

Deeping closed the file and hung his head.

Kell continued: 'I assume Mia Beckhert is someone who you know quite well?'

A muttered "Yes" was all the reply Deeping could manage.

'You see how that when Mia is on reception she's always the one who has checked in the guests who end up being robbed? The only exception to this is when you personally check them in, although she is always on the duty roster for reception when you do. I didn't appreciate that a general manager's duties included reception work.'

Deeping looked up; he clearly wanted to get everything off his chest: 'It wasn't supposed to go that far. Mia and I started to become close, too close in fact and things, you know, developed. We'd use unoccupied rooms and, well, things got out of hand. She liked the finer things in life, fancy clothes and shoes, top restaurants, the works and I couldn't afford it. One day I was chatting to her on reception when this guest came in and Mia noticed he had some fancy Phillipe Patek watch on his wrist.' He paused and took out a tissue to wipe away the tears that were now falling down his pre-jowly cheeks.

'That was the start of it. She went into the rooms in the middle of the night, dressed in a maid's uniform, and just picked up what was lying around. No one woke and the plan was that if they did, she would feign some misunderstanding. She'd then sell on the stuff she didn't want to keep.'

The phone ringing on his desk broke the ensuing silence; he picked it up, said, 'Okay,' and put it back down.

A minute later, two policemen came into his office; Kell nodded to them: 'He's all yours. Have you picked up Miss Beckhert?'

'Yes sir, and thank you for your help.'

Kell left them to it and headed back to the office hoping that Molly had turned up.

There were three messages on the answer machine none of which were from Molly. He hadn't had a text or email giving any indication as to what was wrong so maybe she'd just decided to leave and was too embarrassed to face him, but that wasn't the Molly he knew. She was more likely to ask him for a pay rise after only a few weeks into the job than to just pick up sticks and leave without a word. He rang her mobile again and left another message deciding he'd wait until the morning before involving the authorities.

He was packing away his files, getting ready to head home for the evening when the intercom from the street entry door buzzed.

'Hello, how can I help you?'

'Is that Justin, Justin Kell?' said a young-sounding female voice.

'Yes, it is. Who's that?'

'My name is Lucinda, I'm a friend of Molly. Is she there?'

'You better come up. Just push the door when the buzzer sounds.'

Thirty seconds later, Lucinda Pass was sitting in Kell's office clutching a cup of tea.

'So how long have you been flatmates?' asked Kell.

'We were in the same Halls at Uni and then shared a house with two other girls in our second and third years. We both went travelling, but not together. When we got back I got my job first and the apartment in Leytonstone. It was always the plan for Mol to move in once she got a job; it really helps with the rent and the bills.'

'What is it you do Lucinda?' asked Kell.

'Please, everyone calls me Luci, with an i. I'm in the Compliance team at a financial planning firm. Just a junior, but there's lots of scope for promotion. I really like it, but not as much as Mol loves working here. I can't shut her up about it when she gets home after work.'

'But she didn't come home last night or ring you or leave a message on your phone?'

'No, and that's not like Mol at all. We both always let each other know what we're doing, when we'll be home, especially if one of us is going to be late.'

'And you haven't had any falling out, anything that's caused an upset?' Kell was full-on in his police come private investigator mode. He needed the full picture so he could decide the best course of action.

Luci hesitated before replying. 'Well, she's very taken with you, Justin. She wouldn't shut up about how gorgeous you are. A real man, she called you, nothing like the lads we've both dated over the years. I told her she was playing with fire and that you were far too old for her, sorry about that, but she wouldn't listen insisting she was going to ask you out for a drink. We had a minor argument about it all but nothing serious. Anyway, all her stuff is still in the flat.'

Kell waited to make sure she'd finished before speaking. 'I am far too old for her and I'm living with Amy who I love very much. Molly did flirt with me a bit yesterday evening but nothing blatant. I did my best to ignore it and she seemed okay. So from what you've said, I doubt this has anything to do with her disappearance.'

'Can you find her? I mean you are a private detective. You must find missing persons all the time.' There was a tone of desperation in her voice which sounded the way he felt.

'I'll do what I can, of course, I will. I have contacts in the police who I know will assist. But unless there's a suspicion of foul play, there's only so much time and effort they'll commit to finding her. Let's hope she turns up this evening. If not, I'll call my friend in the Met and get them onto it. I'll start by retracing her steps, this evening and seeing if anyone recognises her. I've got a photo in her personnel file which I can start to show around. She sent me an email at just before seven last night, so she must have left here just after that. This gives us a solid starting point for a timeline, so with all the CCTV that we now have in London, it shouldn't be too hard to trace her movements.'

'So what do you want me to do?' Luci's voice was almost a whisper.

'Just go home and wait. I know it won't be easy, but you never know when she might turn up. If she does, ring me straight away. Here's my card, it's got my mobile number on it. Come on I'll walk you to the station.'

Chapter 21

Molly felt like she was emerging from the deepest sleep she had ever had. She had the mother of all headaches and her nose felt like it was separated from her body. However, no matter how bad the pain was, her journey back to consciousness was awash with relief as she left her nightmares behind.

She tentatively moved her hand to her face to check out the damage to her nose and found she had a manacle around her wrist that was chained to a metal ring in the floor. She automatically tried her other hand and found it secured in exactly the same way.

'Welcome to Hell,' said a voice from the other side of the dimly lit basement. 'I'm Gary Jones, pleased to make your acquaintance.'

Molly slowly got to her feet and turned around to see who had spoken. Her head felt like it was going to split in two and she almost lost her balance. She had a vague recollection that she'd heard that name somewhere before, but her mind was swimming and it wouldn't come to her.

'I'm Molly, and where are we? Why are we tied up like criminals?' She sat back down and lent against the wall to stop herself from fainting.

'The guy is a nutter. Completely barking mad. He's on some sort of mission to get back at the people who've crossed him over the years. I don't know much more than that, he doesn't pop in for afternoon tea so we can have a long chat.'

Molly looked closely at the man sitting on the opposite side of the room. 'God, you look awful, how long have you been here?'

'It's hard to tell. Being down here you get no sense of whether it's day or night, but I've been trying to track time by just sleeping when I think it's night. I can't be certain but I'd say it's about four days.'

Molly started to cry: 'No, no, no. This can't be happening,' she sobbed.

'Listen, stop that. It won't do you any good. If we're going to get out of here we need to have our wits about us and get the psycho to make a mistake.'

'But who is he and why am I here?' Molly was desperately trying to get her emotions back under control.

'His name is James Dodds and he's an ex-copper. I met him in the Scrubs about seven years ago. I was in there for armed robbery and GBH and one day he arrived to share my cell. You're always a bit wary when you get a newcomer especially one who's a first-timer. They don't know the ropes or understand the pecking order inside, which is really important. The guy just didn't seem quite right. He was involved in people trafficking and the whole operation went tits up. From what I can remember him saying, some undercover cop had infiltrated the gang and blown the thing wide open. What Jimmy Dodds didn't tell anyone though was that he was a bent copper working with the chief constable, or someone high up who was pulling the strings. When this came out, well, you can imagine what we inmates all thought. No one likes a bent copper and, for us old school types, we don't care for people traffickers either.'

Jones paused for a moment, which gave Molly the opportunity to ask the obvious question. 'What happened?'

'Me and a couple of like-minded inmates cut him up. Gave him that scar down the left side of his face. If the guards hadn't stopped us, we'd have probably killed him. So you see, it looks like he's been bearing a grudge all this time. I keep expecting my partners in crime to turn up, not a young thing like you.'

'How did he get you down here? Couldn't you have fought him off?' asked Molly.

'He came over to my manor, Streatham, approached me saying he had this job that he needed a man with my skills on. Initially, I told him to fuck off, but he dropped a couple of names and it was like ten grand for a night's work. In the end, he persuaded me to come here to meet the rest of the team. It wasn't until I got to the top of those steps that I realised something was wrong. He pushed me down and got me all tied up. I managed to give him another scar but this is how I ended up.' He held up his wrists which, unlike Molly's, were shackled together.'

Jones went on: 'I mean it when I say he's completely mad. He's changed his name to Jimmy Skaa and thinks it hilarious. He also has conversations with himself which seem to be how he makes decisions. What do they call it? There's some fancy name for it…'

'Schizophrenia,' said Molly. 'You say his name is Jimmy Skaa?'

'Yes, and he's really proud of it,' replied Jones.

'Then I know why he targeted me,' said Molly as she started to cry again.

By the time Molly had finished telling her story, her headache had started to subside. Jones listened without interruption and it was only when she'd finished that he spoke.

'Sounds like it's your boss he's really after. His name is Justin Kell?'

'Yes,' replied Molly.

'I don't know the name,' mused Jones. 'And the thing is it's all happened too fast for him to go crazy about you not taking his case.'

'Oh no!' said Molly as the penny finally dropped. 'Justin was in the Met a few years ago and he did some work undercover. I did a lot of research on him before I applied for the job. It didn't go into the specifics but the articles I read when he left the force were very complimentary, and I'm sure there was a suggestion that he'd been undercover.'

Jones picked up the line of thought: 'If your man was the undercover cop that broke that trafficking ring, then it's no surprise that he's on Skaa's list.'

Just at that moment, they heard the door at the top of the steps open and watched as their captor made his way into their prison.

'Ah good, you're awake. Has Gary shown you all the facilities?' Skaa did that stupid little snigger that Jones had come to hate.

'What sort of a freak are you Dodds? Trapping an innocent girl in your sick plans. I assume it's because you're not man enough to get her boss down here. You're pathetic; you know that, don't you?'

Skaa's demeanour changed instantly.

'My name is Skaa, not Dodds you little prick! You must call me by my proper name!' He was shouting so loudly that his voice made a small echo around the room.

Jones stood up and walked as far as his shackles would permit, directly towards his jailer.

'You don't get it to do you?' Jones kept his voice calm and even. 'You're not a proper criminal; you're just a sick fuck who gets off on kidnapping a woman. There is a code you know, a code that says you leave kids and women alone. You broke that code when you were a bent copper and you're breaking it now dragging her into your pathetic little game, just because you aren't man enough to face up to her boss.'

Jones stood defiantly about three feet from a stunned Skaa, staring him down.

It was Skaa who blinked first and the shock of being confronted in such a considered manner sent him into a frenzy.

'You are going to die!' he screamed. He started to move towards Jones, but at the last second realised he had no weapon and would likely get killed if he got involved in a struggle with his manacled prisoner. He watched in slow motion as Jones swung his secured wrists at his head only to feel the disturbing air brush across his face.

'Calm down, you fool. Calm down or you'll get yourself killed.'

'No, I won't calm down! Stop telling me what to do. I'm going to kill him, kill them both and I'm going to do it now!' With that, he turned and stormed back up the steps.

Jones and Molly stared at one another, 'Who was he talking to?' asked Molly.

'God knows, I reckon it's the other half of his schizo mind. Now we need to be ready when he comes back down. This is likely to be the best chance we have to escape.'

Back upstairs in his living room, Skaa was slowly getting his breathing back under control.

'I'm going to kill that bastard right now and don't you try to stop me!'

'Okay I understand, but you mustn't let him get close to you. You'll have to use the gun.'

'But that won't be any fun! I want him to suffer a slow and agonising death and I want her to watch.'

'In that case, just wound him. I'm not sure you're capable of an accurate shot because of the state you're in. But if you can wound him, then you should be able to have your fun as well.'

Skaa got the gun from the cupboard under the kitchen sink and checked the magazine.

Jones was speaking urgently: 'We have to get him close enough to one of us so we can club him with our chains. I don't know what he's going to do, but we need to calm him down and get him talking, then maybe we have a chance.' His tone was earnest but calm.

'I know what I can do,' said Molly and started to unbutton her blouse.

'Good idea, but if he gets in the range, don't hesitate to club him and keep on clubbing him until he stops moving.'

They looked over to the steps as they heard Skaa return.

'You've pushed me too far this time, Gary. So sadly I'm going to have to bring forward your demise.' He raised the gun and smiled. 'It will hopefully be just a flesh wound, so I can make sure you die a slow and agonising death.'

'Don't you want to have a bit of fun first Jimmy?' said Molly in the most alluring voice she could manage.

Skaa turned towards her as she unclipped her bra and let it hang loosely over her breasts.

For a split second, they both thought he would take the bait as his eyes widened in surprise and he let his arm holding the gun drop to his side.

'Thank you for the very kind offer, but I think not.'

And in one flowing movement he turned and shot Gary Jones.

Chapter 22

Mignemi finished the call from Santini and sat in his West London apartment reading the notes he had taken. He smiled to himself, wondering just how much of what his friend had told him was true and how much was make-believe.

The pace of the operation was speeding up. He could feel it in his bones and his instinct told him that it would likely be only a matter of days before his fate would be decided one way or another. He picked up his phone and dialled Bistro, the restaurant in a quiet part of Soho, and booked a table for 7:30 that evening.

He passed the afternoon reading a book on Greek mythology. He'd been fascinated by the subject ever since he'd taken it as an option for his studies at secondary school and was always on the lookout for books or manuscripts that provided a different insight or perspective. However, that afternoon his mind kept drifting to the series of events that had transpired to put his life in the gravest of danger. He accepted he made a mistake with Henry Gray; the man didn't have the backbone or the greed to see the job through. But it was the interference of the reporter Justin Kell, whose instincts and relentless pursuit of the truth had brought the downfall of the Horizon operation and his friend Bobby Dulac. In many ways he admired Kell, he was exactly the type of man he could see himself working with. Of course, that wouldn't stop him from killing him when the time came but he respected the man for the truth and justice he stood for. He'd done his research and seen that Kell had left the newspaper and had set himself up as some sort of freelance journalist come private investigator. He had the address of his office and planned to drop by and see him as soon as matters with Aljadid were more stable.

He put down his book and turned on the evening television. The lead story on BBC London News was of a young woman who had gone missing on her way home from work. She was last seen getting on the Eastbound Central Line at Liverpool Street. There was a live report from Leytonstone Underground station where the woman in question was supposed to get off, but the vandalism of the CCTV cameras meant there was no confirmation. He looked at his watch and decided he better get moving as he planned to walk down to the restaurant as it was a pleasant early summer evening. He was about to switch off the TV when a familiar face filled the screen. He listened with interest before putting the set onto standby and heading off for the most important meal of his life, but with sadly little appetite.

He arrived at the Bistro just after 7:30 and was greeted with a warm smile by the receptionist who showed him to a table that was on its own at the side of the bar. She left the menu and moments later, a carafe of water and a plate of small slices of bread and oils were delivered. He ordered spiced sea bass with rice and vegetables and a small glass of the recommended house wine.

When the waitress arrived to take his plate he complimented the quality of the food but declined to see the dessert menu and asked for the bill. He was surprised he hadn't had any company but wasn't going to ask if Alex was on the premises.

'Are you sure there's nothing else you want, Alfio?'

He looked up to see a smiling Alex walking towards him from behind the bar.

'Maybe we could share something?' replied Mignemi.

'Then please, let's go somewhere more comfortable.'

He led him through a door at the side of the bar and up a narrow flight of stairs to a landing with two doors on each side. He went to the second door on the right, knocked, and waited for the command to enter.

'So, am I finally meeting someone who calls the shots?' asked Mignemi.

Before Alex could reply a voice from the other side of the door said 'Enter'. Alex led him into a room that was furnished in a modern style with leather sofas and chairs surrounding a large coffee table. A man and woman of similar age to Alex stood by a drinks cabinet and watched as they walked in.

There was no warm welcome, no smiles, no handshakes, the couple just stood where they were sipping their drinks.

Finally, the woman spoke: 'Thank you Alex, you may leave us.'

Alex dutifully left the room, leaving Mignemi waiting for an introduction.

Again it was the woman who broke the silence: 'Please sit down Mr Mignemi,' she said gesturing to one of the sofas. The man put down his drink and sat directly opposite their guest. The woman sat on the sofa to Mignemi's right making it so he would have to constantly turn his head if he wanted to look at them both while speaking.

'We have differing views on whether it is worth meeting with you, Alfio,' it was the man who now spoke. 'We find it difficult to believe your story,' he paused, 'but then again, why would you put yourself in such a position if you were not being honest with us?'

'I'm not going to repeat my position for the third time,' he replied. 'If you are not interested in my proposal, then I will leave and our paths will never cross again.'

It was the woman's turn to reply: 'Irrespective of the value of your information, we cannot give you what you want. We are two of the Al Khamsa. Five families rule the Aljadid and five it must stay. You will understand the value and power of the five. So there is no way you could join the Al Khamsa even when we succeed in bringing down the Qadim, with or without your help.'

Mignemi had prepared for such an outcome. The Maktab knew that a seat at the top table wouldn't just be given away for some snippets of useful information.

'I understand that completely. But when I have shared my information, I hope you will see the value I could be as an adviser to the Al Khamsa.'

'I'm not sure we need your advice Alfio,' this time the man with no name spoke. It was clear they simply operated as a tag team.

Mignemi reached into his inside pocket and drew out a folded sheet of A4 paper. He held it up towards them, turning it so they could both see both sides were full of a handwritten script.

'This side gives the details of a Qadim cell in Germany that is on the verge of breaking away and, how shall I put it, going independent. My view is they don't have the scale to be anything but an insignificant local gang. However, with the benefit of an influential master, there is plenty of scope for them to be a valuable part of an organisation like yours.'

He turned the paper over.

'These are the details of the next two meetings of the Maktab. They meet every month at one of the companies they use to launder their money. They are all export businesses, chemical, tobacco, paper, construction, even wine. They meet next at the weekend; this should give you sufficient time to verify that what I say is true. If you are then satisfied as to where my loyalties lie, I can assist you in removing the Maktab permanently, potentially as soon as within four weeks' time.'

The man and woman with no names did not acknowledge that he had finished speaking. They did not even look at one another. After what he estimated must have been five minutes, the woman stood up and held out her hand. 'Thank you Alfio, we will evaluate what you have provided and will be in touch if we have further need of you.' She shook his hand as did the man who had walked to his side of the table.

The door opened and Alex showed him out.

Back in the room, the man and woman read the paper that had been left on the coffee table.

'If this checks out, then maybe we can find a role for Mr Mignemi after all,' said the woman.

'Indeed we may. Shall we have a drink to celebrate?' replied the man.

Chapter 23

The following morning Kell got to the office just after 7:00 am. His vain hope that Molly would have turned up and come in early to make up for the time she missed yesterday vanished as soon he realised that she wasn't there.

He went through the usual morning rituals of opening up his laptop and making himself a coffee but his mind simply wouldn't function. When it got to 8:00, he rang Chis Packham on his mobile.

When the call connected he was greeted with: 'Good morning early bird. Didn't realise you knew what eight o'clock in the morning looked like.'

Kell didn't bother with any banter: 'It's Molly, she missing and I think she's been abducted.'

Packham's tone changed immediately: 'When did you last see her?'

'When I left the office two nights ago to come and meet you. She didn't come into work yesterday and she isn't answering her phone. Her flatmate came to the office yesterday evening to see if I knew where she was. She hasn't been back to her flat for two nights and the only clothes she's got are what she came to work in two days ago.'

'Right, give me all of the details, name, address and description, and I'll pass them onto our misper team. I'll make sure they are at your office within an hour. It would also save time if you could get her flatmate there as well.' Packham was just about to hang up: 'Oh, I almost forgot. I've got some interesting news on the Llubovs, but it can wait till later.'

Kell gave his friend Molly's details and then rang Luci and asked her if she could come to the office to give the police a statement. Then he sat back and waited.

Less than an hour later, two policewomen arrived at Kell's office and he repeated everything he could about the last time he'd seen Molly. No, she hadn't been acting strangely, no he wasn't aware of any boyfriend issues, but her flatmate was on her way and would be a better person to ask, yes the standard of her work was excellent, yes she settled in well and so it went on. At some point in the questioning, he started to feel like he was a suspect until he told them that he'd been with DI Chris Packham that evening.

He gave them her picture that he'd shown around yesterday evening to commuters pouring into Liverpool Street station, but most hardly even glanced at it, and he soon realised it was a pointless exercise.

Luci arrived an hour later and the policewomen repeated the same questions they'd asked Kell. Luci was able to tell them that Molly's parents lived on the south coast somewhere, Worthing, she thought it was, but she didn't have a number so hadn't checked if she'd gone there. The police advised they would take care of that and get their permission to go to the media to ask for information.

'Mr Kell, are you okay if we use the details of where she worked? It will help with confirming her movements along with any CCTV footage of sightings?'

'Yes of course and please, call me Justin.'

The policewomen gave him a sympathetic smile: 'Of course, thank you, Justin. We will try to get the appeal for information on the lunchtime news, but it will definitely be on the evening slot. With such a defined window for the CCTV review, we should have something concrete by then.'

When the policewomen had left, Kell made Luci another cup of coffee and they just sat there deep in their own thoughts. Eventually, it was Luci who broke the uneasy silence.

'She's been abducted, hasn't she? Do you think she's still alive? Don't they say that unless you find a missing person in the first forty-eight hours then the odds are they're dead?'

'Come on now. There's no need to think like that. We must keep positive and let the police do their job.' Kell tried to sound as convincing as possible but was pretty sure that he failed miserably.

As Luci was preparing to leave, the door intercom buzzed. Kell pressed the button, 'Yes?'

'It's Chris, are you free for half an hour?'

Kell buzzed him in. Luci looked hopefully at him and asked: 'Is he a policeman? Will he have some news?'

'Yes, he is a policeman, but I expect he wants to discuss another case I'm working on. You get to work and I'll let you know if there are any developments.'

Kell did cursory introductions as Luci lingered by the door as though waiting for an invitation to stay.

Kell gave her a hug and said: 'Get back to work Luci, I promise I'll keep in touch.'

She reluctantly left leaving the two men alone.

'I know this a difficult time Justin, but let us do our job and I'm sure we'll find her.'

Kell slumped into one of the chairs around the meeting table and gestured for Packham to do the same.

'Yes I know, it's just that I feel responsible. Anyway, what brings you down here, it must be something important to drag you out of your cushy office?'

Packham stood and went to make himself a cup of coffee. 'Do you want one?'

'No thanks, and please make yourself at home.'

Packham was encouraged that his friend still had a bit of banter in him. He made his coffee and sat back down at the table.

'There's been a significant development in the Llubov case.'

Kell leant forward his interest immediately focussed on what the DI had to say, all worries about Molly momentarily forgotten.

Packham continued: 'They requested a meeting with the liaison officer. She works for us, her name is Maja Sech. Bright young thing, came through the graduate programme, multi-lingual etc, etc. Anyway, following the meeting which lasted over an hour, she reported back that our psycho friends had given her the name of Wirebound Electronics.'

Kell couldn't help but interrupt: 'But that's the firm Mignemi went and visited and you're pretty sure it's an Aljadid front?'

'The very same one. But the thing is they told the lovely Maja that it's a Qadim company and it was likely that our friend Alfio would be operating out of there.'

Packham sat back smiling and put his hands behind his head giving him that "aren't I so clever look".

Kell looked puzzled: 'But it doesn't make any sense!'

'Exactly! Don't you see the Llubovs know nothing? They don't have any Intel at all. Whatever they give us comes from our double-crossing little bitch Maja Sech!'

Kell was nodding: 'It's so obvious, isn't it? She tells the Llubovs what going on so there's consistency down the line if it's needed and her "real" bosses just feed us the information they want to. Leading us off the scent, sending you guys on wild goose chases, down rabbit holes, or whatever other metaphor you want to use. But the question is, why?'

'We had a late briefing last night, finished at midnight and the view is that they're simply buying time.'

'Buying time for what?' asked Kell.

'Until the time is right for the Qadim to have a go at rescuing the Llubovs.'

'Okay, makes sense, but what are you going to do about whatshername?'

Packham scratched his head. 'There are mixed views. One is to suspend her, charge her with perverting the course of justice, take her into custody, and see what she's prepared to spill on her masters. The other is to leave her be and see if any further Intel helps us. You remember what your friend Smithe said about the different factions of the Security Services being involved?'

'Yes.'

'Well, that's what's holding up the decision. My guess is that our chief constable will win the day and she'll be taken into custody. She is after all one of his staff. If I'm right, then as soon as this happens it will flag up that we're onto them and could potentially force the Qadim's hand if they want to try to spring the Llubovs.'

'I thought you said they had implants that track exactly where they are?' asked Kell.

'They do, but it's straight forward to remove them if they have the right equipment. And my guess is that this is where Mignemi will show his hand.'

'What will they do to the Llubovs, assuming that they remain in custody?'

Packham replied: 'There's every chance they'll be retried, or should I say their original trial is reconvened. Once the decision on Sech is made, everything will happen quickly. We've already beefed up the security on them, so any breakout attempt is likely to fail.'

Kell stood up and started pacing around the office: 'So what do we do?'

'There's not a lot we can do Justin. It's just like Molly's case; you need to let the authorities get on with their job. At least, it looks like the Llubovs will finally face justice.'

'Where are they being detained again? Where's' the safe house?' Kell raised his eyebrows as he asked the question.

'I don't believe I've shared that information. But seeing it's you, they're in Bermondsey.' Packham got out his pen and scribbled the address on a piece of scrap paper.

'Now I've got to go. I'll keep abreast of the hunt for Molly and will keep in touch if anything breaks.'

'Thanks, Chris. I'm going to mull over what you've told me and see if there's anything I can do to assist.

Packham didn't respond, he just shook his head as he left.

Chapter 24

Skaa stood stock still staring at the body of Gary Jones lying in a pool of his own blood. The noise of the shot had echoed around the basement and Molly stared at the body with wide eyes and her hands over her ears.

Eventually, Skaa broke their reverie; 'That'll teach you for being rude to me. Now sit up and let's see how badly you're hurt.'

Jones didn't move but Molly noticed he was still breathing.

'I think he's unconscious,' she said. 'You've got to stop the bleeding otherwise he'll die.'

'Shut up bitch. When I want your advice I'll ask for it.'

'She's right you know. You need to check where the bullet went in, otherwise, he'll bleed out and that wouldn't be any fun would it?'

Skaa walked tentatively to the body and somewhat gingerly turned it over with his foot. Jones did not stir but Molly was dismayed to see his breath was coming in rapid shallow bursts. The bullet appeared to have struck Jones in the chest, just below his right shoulder. The rate of blood loss suggested that a major artery hadn't been severed, but his face was ashen and lifeless.

Skaa put the gun down in the middle of the room doing a quick visual check that Molly couldn't reach it. Then with some effort, he pulled the body up into a sitting position and dragged it so it was propped against the wall. He secured Jones' hands to clips that he had put into the walls which gave his victim a Jesus on the cross-type look. Happy that the prospect of any attack coming from his prisoner was now very unlikely, he set about ripping Jones shirt off and examining the wound.

'It looks like the bullet is still in there, which is fine as it will limit the bleeding. Infection is almost guaranteed but if you clean him up he'll probably live for a couple of days so you can have your fun and make him really suffer.'

'Right, I'll do just that,' and he headed back upstairs to fetch his extensive medical kit.

As soon as he was at the top of the stairs Molly called across the room: 'Gary, Gary are you okay? Can you hear me? You need to wake up.' She kept her voice like a stage whisper but when there was no response she started to shout. 'Gary, wake up!'

'No need to shout my dear, I'll make sure he's conscious for the next part of my plan.' Skaa walked down the steps holding a green first aid box. It was the sort of thing you saw on the wall in a school classroom that contained a few plasters for when one of the kids scraped a knee.

Skaa put it down next to the lifeless body and opened it up. Molly watched as he got out a swab of cotton wool and poured some antiseptic solution onto it and started to wipe away the blood from the wound. He repeated the act with a second swab which cleared the remaining blood from the area. He leaned back to check his work then took a piece of lint from the green box and folded it into four. He then pressed it over the wound and secured it with what looked to Molly like parcel tape.

He stood up, went to the sink, and filled one of the tin cups with water. He put the cup to Jones' mouth and encouraged him to drink.

To Molly's relief, he responded by slowly sipping the water. Skaa rummaged around in the first aid box and found a bottle of pills. He shook out four into his hands and started to feed them to the shackled, broken body.

'There, now that should do it. You'll be feeling right as rain in no time.' Skaa stood up and looked down at his victim.

The pain in Jones' shoulder and chest was excruciating, but he managed to open his eyes and look at his tormenter.

'You're one sick fuck, Jimmy. One sick fuck!'

'I'll take that as a compliment. Thank you, Gary. Now that you're feeling better I think it's time we finally got started. The main event you could say!'

From out of his pocket, he pulled a new looking Stanley knife and slowly pushed out the blade to its maximum length.

Molly screamed as the mad man knelt down next to his manacled victim and started to cut his face to pieces.

'This one is for what you and your cowardly mates did to me,' the knife slid easily through the skin starting at Jones' left eye and cutting down to the corner of his mouth. Jones didn't scream. He did though keep talking, reminding Skaa what a depraved bastard he was.

Skaa seemed not to hear these words or Molly screams that begged for mercy. He simply kept on cutting. He moved the knife next to Jones' right eye.

'This one is for the cut you gave me when you first arrived here,' he sniggered that stupid little laugh that made Molly's blood run cold.

The cut was almost a perfect match of the first but was soon hidden by the steady flow of blood that made Jones' face look like a clown's that was having a bad day.

Skaa stood back up and surveyed his handy work smiling.

'Excellent! I think that went really well, don't you Gary?'

Jones didn't acknowledge the question but kept his eyes firmly fixed on the mad thing towering above him.

'Now then Gary, I don't like that look you're giving me. I don't like it at all.'

'Well don't fucking look at me then,' were the words that came out of Jones' mouth and which proved to be his last.

'I think it's best that you don't look at me actually,' replied Skaa. And with that, he bent down and started to cut out Jones's eyes.

That was when the screaming really did start.

Chapter 25

Santini was sitting in one of the chairs at the gents' hairdressers in the city. Despite the sharp clipping sound the scissors made as the barber moved them around his head, no hair was being removed. Mignemi walked in, sat in the adjacent chair, and waited until he had a cape put around his shoulders before speaking.

'I didn't think you'd need a haircut so soon?' he enquired of the solicitor.

'You may leave us, thank you.' Santini gestured to the men posing as barbers.

The two hairdressers went and stood by the entrance door of the shop which was now closed for business.

He continued: 'Miss Sech has been compromised, suspended and charged with perverting the course of justice. She is being held at Westminster police station and whilst it will be difficult for the authorities to make the charges stick, it exposes the Llubovs to re-arrest. We must, therefore, move quickly to secure their return to the family.'

'My plan is ready to go at any time. Do you have the medicine I asked for?'

Santini reached into his inside pocket and pulled out two small vials in answer to the question.

'I am assured they will perform exactly as requested and the transport is already in place.'

Mignemi gestured to the men guarding the door; one stepped forward and removed the cape draped around his shoulders. 'I assume you can instruct them immediately?'

'Yes, I will go to them straight away. As their solicitor, I do not need an appointment.'

'Good. Tell them to go out for lunch to the café they frequent, just before you get into the town centre. Inform them to start the performance at 1:00 pm sharp. All being well, we will see you at the farmhouse in Essex by late afternoon.'

The solicitor just nodded and both men left together.

Andrei Llubov and his sister were getting worried. They had been in the "safe house" for three weeks and their instincts were telling them that things were not going well.

They had had only two meetings with Maja, the liaison officer, and she had not provided any encouragement that their detention, which is how they saw it, would be over soon. The meeting yesterday had been particularly disappointing.

'I cannot believe that all we are supposed to have provided to the authorities is the name of some shell company that is supposedly used by the Qadim. It doesn't make any sense, particularly as Maja tells us it's actually an Aljadid front!'

'Calm down Andrei, we just need to sit tight. I'm sure they know what they are doing.' replied his sister.

'But we're supposed to be giving intelligence on a major operation that's about to go down! They must realise by now that we don't know anything and if Maja gets rumbled, then we're in real trouble. If we get questioned by anyone else, the best we can hope for is to end up back in court.'

'Look, as soon as we think our situation is untenable, we'll run. I've been through the plan with you countless times.' Darya was not used to her brother being so unnerved. They had been in far worse situations than this and had always found a way out. The implanted tracking devices might be a minor inconvenience but she was sure that could be overcome.

'Come on, let's go out for an early lunch and see how obvious our surveillance is today.'

As they were putting their coats on, there was a knock at the door. When she opened it, she was surprised to see Santini and, standing just behind him, a man she recognised as one of their surveillance team.

'What a nice surprise Miguel! How are you?' She greeted him with a kiss on each cheek.

Santini turned to the officer. 'I just need five minutes with my clients.'

When the officer did not move, he added: 'In private.'

The man just nodded and made it clear he would be waiting right outside the door and would make sure that five minutes was just that and not a second longer.

As soon as the door was shut, Darya led them into the small kitchen where her brother was waiting. Santini did not sit down or wait to be asked if he wanted a coffee before handing the two vials to the female sibling and explaining what they needed to do. He did not ask if they had any questions and less than three minutes after he entered the house on a quiet street in Bermondsey he was leaving, nodding to the police officer standing outside as he left.

At the same time when the Llubovs were greeting their unexpected visitor, Mignemi was back in his apartment in Chiltern Street changing into a uniform that would make even a close friend look twice to check it was him. By the time he added a baseball type cap that was part of the official outfit he could have been anyone. He checked himself in the mirror and gave a nod of satisfaction at the completeness of the disguise. He left the apartment and took the service lift down to the garage where his vehicle was waiting with the crew already on board. He checked his watch, 11:55, plenty of time to get across the river and into place.

He climbed into the back of the vehicle: 'Right let's go.'

Andrei and Darya Llubov were professionals. Army trained, with a discipline that meant they did not question any order they were given. They walked to their lunch destination in silence and deep in thought with the prospect of impending freedom. They forced down the implications of what would happen if things went wrong. They arrived at the restaurant come café just after 12:30. They were regulars and were greeted warmly by the waitress who seated them. They both ordered salads one with seafood and one with chicken. As usual, the service was very efficient and their lunch arrived five minutes later. Darya checked her watch. The digital display showed 12:44. Perfect, everything was on track.

The officer from the surveillance team who had escorted the solicitor to their front door sat in the same unmarked police car on the opposite side of the road thirty yards from the restaurant. The road was part of the one-way system and he had a clear sight of the entrance in his rear-view mirror. He was relaxed. This was the same routine as most days and the screen set into the dashboard showed his charges ninety-eight feet away and stationary. He'd been told to escort their bent solicitor into the house and whilst he was slightly unnerved by the shortness of the meeting he'd not reported back that he'd lost visual contact for what must have been less than four minutes. Anyway, no harm, no foul. He took another bite of his pastrami sandwich and kept his eyes flitting between the entrance of the café and the screen on the dashboard.

When her watch showed 12:59, Darya Llubov took the vials Santini had provided and checked that she selected the one with the red label. She moved her hand across the table as if to touch her brother in a show of affection and passed it to him. He moved both his hands to below the table and looked at his sister.

When the display on her watch changed to 13:00, she nodded to her brother. He downed the contents on the vial and returned the empty ampoule to her.

Less than thirty seconds later, his pupils began to dilate and then he started fitting. Darya screamed and went to her brother. 'Call an ambulance, he's having a fit. Somebody call an ambulance!'

It was the barista who made the call and then hurried to the other side of the counter where he joined the rest of the customers who had gathered in a semi-circle around the man who was having what everyone thought was an epileptic fit.

In the unmarked police car thirty yards down the road, the surveillance officer had just finished his sandwich and was opening a bag of salt and vinegar crisps. The screen on the dashboard showed that his charges had not moved. Moments later he became aware of the sirens of an ambulance. Not an unusual sound on the streets of London but this one was getting close, and something about it didn't feel right. He checked the entrance to the café again and noted that the screen did not indicate anything other than the Llubovs were still enjoying their lunch.

He turned in his seat as the noise of the ambulance grew to a crescendo and saw it pull up outside the café. Instinctively, he got out of the car and ran to see if there was anything he could do to assist. At this point, he wasn't concerned about the brother and sister, after all, they couldn't get far with no transport and the trackers firmly embedded in their upper arms.

He got to the entrance as the paramedics were wheeling out a man who was fitting. His eyes were wide, the pupils expanding and contracting as if they were breathing and he was foaming at the mouth. It was only when the female walking alongside the stretcher turned to him and said: 'Please can you clear the traffic and lead us to the hospital, I don't think he has much time.'

Of all the mistakes he made that day, this was the one that cost him his job and busted him back to pounding the beat.

'Of course, I'll get the blues and twos going.' He ran back to his car and pulled out into the one-way street.

The ambulance doors slammed shut and it pulled away with sirens blaring. In the intervening seconds, a car had managed to put itself between the unmarked police car and the ambulance but the officer was certain it would move out of the way as soon as the driver realised he was the meat in the sandwich of an emergency.

Inside the ambulance Mignemi, dressed in the green uniform of a paramedic, took control.

'Pass me the second vial Darya.'

She handed it to him as he steadied himself against the movement of the vehicle and inserted a syringe into the liquid fully extracting its contents. He didn't check the amount or spray a little into the air like they did in the medical shows on television; he simply pushed the needle into the fitting man's arm and emptied the contents without hesitation.

He put the empty syringe to one side and nodded to one of the other two men in the back of the ambulance. 'Your arm please Darya. Hendrick will remove the tracker.'

The instability of an ambulance travelling at as high a speed as the London traffic would allow did not appear to phase the young man Mignemi had called Hendrick from identifying the small scar on the woman's upper arm and carefully slicing it open with a scalpel. He then took what looked like one of those corkscrews that fit onto a bottle and as you turn it the two arms rise up so you can then push them down to extract the cork. But instead of a screw, the implement had what looked like a small bulldog clip at the end.

'This will hurt, but the device will be out in a matter of seconds.'

Hendrick placed the device over the incision and started to turn the handle. Darya grimaced in pain as what she thought of as the bulldog clip slowly opened pushing aside her flesh as it entered her arm. It seemed a lot longer than the matter of seconds that had been promised but as the handle was turned the other way to secure its grip on the microchip, the pain started to subside, and slowly the offending object was extracted.

'Please clean up the wound,' Hendrick requested the other man and turned his attention to the male patient, who was no longer fitting and starting to breathe normally as he slowly regained consciousness. He repeated the procedure and passed the chip to Mignemi who had just finished placing the first one into one end of a white plastic tube that was forty centimetres long with a two centimetre diameter. He placed the second chip in the other end and passed it to the man riding shotgun in the front cab.

The surveillance officer had assumed that the ambulance would go to Guy's hospital as even in heavy traffic it should be no more than ten minutes away. For some reason, the car separating him from the ambulance had not pulled over but he was reassured that the screen still showed both trackers fifty yards behind him. He had been to this hospital on countless occasions throughout his career and didn't need to follow the signs directing him to A&E. He turned onto the hospital approach and wasn't surprised that the car that had accompanied him all the way from the cafe followed. After all, they were probably going there as well. However, when the ambulance did not follow, he did a double-take of the mental picture he had of the surrounding area and his momentary panic subsided when he realised that they were probably heading to Emergency Admissions.

As soon as the surveillance turned off towards the A&E entrance, the ambulance pulled over and a white plastic tube was passed to the rider of a motor scooter who put it in the box behind the seat and set off for the Emergency Admissions entrance.

The ambulance pulled away, no sirens now needed and headed down Stamford Street towards Waterloo Bridge. Less than a mile later they turned off the main road and headed south, away from the city.

The real ambulance arrived at the café/restaurant in Bermondsey precisely seven minutes after the 999 call was logged. The crew could not understand how the emergency had been answered by another responder and checked back with the control room. When they confirmed that none of the other crews in the area had been assigned to the call the mystery was referred to the shift supervisor. At a time when resources were stretched and most of the team were having to pull double shifts, he decided to just log it, which would automatically keep a record in the shift report. By the time anyone put two and two together, it would be far too late.

They left the ambulance in a back street garage in Peckham and Hendrick, Mignemi and the Llubovs transferred to a Ford Transit van that had been modified to seat up to nine people in the back.

As they headed off down the A2 to get to the Dartford Crossing, Mignemi broke the silence: 'Welcome back to the free world comrades. If the traffic is kind we should be in time for afternoon tea with your solicitor and the briefing for your next assignment.'

The police found the trackers in a waste bin just outside the entrance of Emergency Admissions at Guy's hospital. All available operational personnel was scrambled to find the missing ambulance, but with no real belief that they would.

Chapter 26

The converted Transit van arrived at the farmhouse at 3:45. The sun was shining and it was pleasantly warm as Mignemi, the Llubovs and Hendrick walked across the courtyard to be greeted by a smiling Santini.

'Excellent, you made it. I assume the operation went smoothly?'

It was Mignemi who replied: 'Like clockwork. No concerns, no clues left behind. Everyone did their job.'

'Come, let us go inside and have some tea. We have a lot to discuss.' Santini led them through the kitchen to what was the front of the house and onto a small terrace where tea, coffee, and a range of sandwiches had been set out.

'Please sit and help yourselves.'

There was clearly a pecking order as the three younger members of the party waited for Mignemi and Santini to sit down before doing so themselves and it was Hendrick who said: 'Allow me. Miguel, Alfio would you like tea or coffee?'

When the drinks had been poured, it was Mignemi who spoke first.

'I am in the process of infiltrating the highest echelon of the Aljadid. I have provided them with certain information, which once they check out will hopefully confirm that I am serious about bringing down the Qadim by helping them arrange the slaughter of the Maktab. I have already met two of their so-called "High Command", a man and a woman who represent two of five families that rule their organisation. They imaginatively call themselves Al Khamsa, which is simply a translation of "The Five" from an Arabic dialect.'

When he paused Santini spoke: 'Are you happy for our friends to ask questions as you take us through your plan Alfio?'

'Yes, of course.'

It was Hendrick who asked the obvious question: 'And once you have infiltrated the Aljadid's High Command, I assume it's your intention that we kill them?'

Mignemi smiled: 'It is indeed. I need to gather more details before I can finalise the plan but I expect it will involve you accompanying me to their headquarters and being quicker on the draw than they are.'

Santini let this image sink in before interjecting: 'In the meantime, you three will stay here out of sight of the authorities and what is probably going to be a full-scale manhunt for you two.' He looked at the Llubovs who had not said anything since arriving at the farmhouse.

'Once Alfio has finalised the arrangements to remove the Aljadid from the face of the earth, we will arrange for the three of you to go back to Beirut.'

'Now, I must change my clothes and get back to London. The fact I was off the radar at the same time that you escaped, will have been noticed by my admirers.' Mignemi walked back into the house and went to the bedroom he'd used on his previous visit and changed into his day to day uniform of a three-piece suit, white shirt, and plain tie.

His journey back to London was uneventful. He got out of the car opposite Madame Tussauds and walked down to his apartment building. He was not surprised to see a familiar-looking Bentley waiting outside. As he approached, the vehicle drove off. He turned to watch it go, instantly seeing the reason for its hasty departure. Two plainclothes police officers were walking towards him. He recognised one of them from the time he was arrested in relation to the Horizon debacle and at the subsequent trial, the other he did not.

They didn't bother showing their IDs. The man he recognised took the lead: 'Hello Alfio, we've been looking everywhere for you. Can we come in and have a little chat?'

'Yes of course Mr…I recognise the face but can't put a name to it.'

'It's DI Packham, and this is my colleague, Mr Smith.'

'Ah, a joint effort from the police and the security service. Something must be very important?'

He led them into the reception, nodded to the man on the desk, and pressed the button to call the lift. As they entered the apartment, Mignemi asked: 'Would you like tea or coffee? I assume that as you are on duty I cannot tempt you with anything stronger?'

Packham took the lead: 'Nothing for us, thank you. We are rather busy at the moment.'

'Very well, please sit.' He gestured to the settee which provided a stunning view of the London skyline.

Packham continued: 'Where were you this afternoon from one o'clock until we met you just now.'

'Let me see. I had my lunch here and as it was such a pleasant afternoon I went for a walk in Regents Park. After that, I went to the British Library. I got immersed in one of the books I was reading and lost all track of time. I left there about forty minutes ago and walked back here.'

'And what book was it that you were so immersed in?' asked the DI.

'It was a book on the origins of Lebanese culture written in the 19th century by little known philosopher, Burclee.' Mignemi smiled and turned his head slightly as if to say do you really think I would be tripped up by such a stupid question?

Packham changed tack: 'Do you know a Maja Sech?'

'It is not a name I am familiar with.'

'Are you sure, Alfio? She works for the same organisation that you do.'

'And which organisation is that?'

'The same one that organised the Horizon Settlement Fund scandal. The same one that pays the rent on this very nice apartment. The same one that you've been working for your entire adult life.'

'I am retired now, Mr Packham. Please can't you just leave me in peace?'

Mr Smith finally broke his silence: 'We'll check out your story, Mr Mignemi. If we can't find you on any of the CCTV cameras between here and Regents Park or any of the scores of cameras throughout the British Library then I can assure you that you won't be enjoying such pleasant views for a long, long time.'

'And what would you be charging me with?'

'Oh, there'll be no charge. You will simply disappear like you did today and none of your gangster friends will have a clue where you are.'

Both men got up and left the apartment. The good mood that had been with him all day had been quickly been replaced by a sense of inevitable darkness. Whatever happened, he doubted the ending would be a happy one for him.

Fifteen minutes after the policemen left, reception rang and told him his car was outside.

As he waited for the lift, he asked himself was it all worth it? He was exposed on all sides. The Qadim, the Aljadid, and the security services. One of them was bound to get him, but which one? Maybe it was time he started to look after number one.

Alex was waiting for him, leaning against the Bentley.

'Good evening, Alfio. How was your day?'

'Interesting, thank you Alex. You obviously didn't want to stay and have a chat with my visitors?'

They got in the car and it drove off. Alex didn't answer the question straight away and the silence in the car was unnerving Mignemi.

Eventually, the Aljadid gofer spoke: 'I imagine they asked you the same questions that I will now ask. Where were you this afternoon, and why did you sneak out of your apartment?'

'I didn't sneak out as you put it, Alex. I went for a walk in Regents Park and then spent the rest of the afternoon at the British Library. Because I was heading that way, it's quicker to use the staff entrance at the back of the building. You are correct that the policemen asked the same questions but they didn't say why. You must realise that I'm not very popular with them as I recently escaped their clutches.'

'Very well. But if you are to work for us, there can be no sneaking around out of our sight. The first sign of trouble and we will kill you Alfio. So please be very careful from now on.'

He didn't respond to the warning, but the sense of foreboding got a little more intense.

Lost in his own thoughts, he wasn't paying attention to where they were heading. The traffic was heavy and they'd been driving for forty-five minutes when they drove past Notting Hill tube station. A right then a left turn later, the car turned into an underground car park below a grand Victorian building that was typical in the Holland Park area.

Two men stood on either side of the entrance and waved them through once they recognised the car and its occupants. The car went down the ramp and turned into a spacious area that was about half full of top of the range vehicles. The driver parked in a space next to a door that was "guarded" by a man who was clearly wearing a shoulder holster beneath his Armani suit. The driver got out and stood by his door and watched as Mignemi and Alex emerged from the car. The guard nodded a "hello", turned, and opened the door, which led into a small alcove with a set of stairs and the door to a lift which was already open. They got in, Alex pressed 2 and they began their short ascent.

'What is on the other two floors?' he asked.

'This is a private members' club. We have a bar and restaurant on the ground floor and an exclusive casino on the first. It only gets used once every fortnight when we host a special event. Usually a poker game, but there is also roulette and blackjack.'

The lift doors opened and his minder led him on down a carpeted corridor to a set of double doors at the end. He knocked and was immediately told to enter. Mignemi was not surprised to see the man and the woman he had met previously sitting on either side of a large boardroom type table sipping glasses of water.

'Thank you Alex. Please could you wait outside?'
'Please Alfio, take a seat.'

He sat down at the head of the table and poured himself a glass of water.

The woman took the lead: 'We have checked out the information you provided Alfio and are very pleased that you were telling the truth. We have contacted the group in Germany and believe we can reach an understanding with them. We also observed the venue where your old masters met and from what we can tell that also seemed to be correct.'

'As I told you, I have no reason to try to mislead you.'

The man then spoke: 'Tell us Alfio, how often the Maktab meet?'

Mignemi chuckled. 'They meet on every full moon. This has nothing to do with the supernatural or any stupid superstitions. It's a tradition they adopted when they realised back in the early days that their first three meetings just so happened to be when the moon was full. They simply decided to keep the tradition going, so everyone knew what was what.'

The woman: 'Very good. So we have certainty on when they will meet next. We would like to move quickly Alfio, so do you know where this meeting will take place?'

'Indeed I do. And I will gladly share this with you and the other members of your executive, once you agree to my terms. I will also give you the information that will make certain you can get past their security and deliver the coup de gras.'

The man and woman looked at each other and he noticed the nod of agreement.

'Very well. On behalf of Al Khamsa, we agree to your terms. We will welcome you to our ranks as soon as we have cut the head off the snake. You will have certain privileges that go with the rank of an adviser to Al Khamsa and enjoy the protection of our organisation.'

She stood up and walked around the table to him. 'Welcome Alfio, my name is Irini and this is Helmut. You will meet the other three one week from tonight when you will brief us on how we will destroy the Maktab and bring down the Qadim. Alex will pick you up at 9:00 pm and you will join the meeting at 10:00. Do you have any questions?

'Thank you Irini, I will not let you down, but I do have one small request to make. There are three of my ex-colleagues who are in a similar position as me but without the benefit of any arrangement with my former employers. They are loyal to me and understand my situation. I would appreciate it if you would let me employ them as my protection team. They are very efficient and will adhere willingly to any terms you require.'

After a short pause to take in the request, it was the man introduced as Helmut who answered the question: 'I understand your nervousness Alfio and am sympathetic to your request. Until we have all established the required element of trust, to have people close to you that you can rely on is only natural. What arrangement do you have in mind?'

'I have my own driver who takes me everywhere and remains with the vehicle at all times. I have two assistants who accompany me wherever I go. So, for next week's meeting, they would escort me here and then wait with the rest of the security detail outside of the room.'

It was Irini's turn to speak: 'It is not an unreasonable demand. I'm sure you'll understand if we instruct our personnel to be extra vigilant in their presence until we are all satisfied we can trust each other completely.'

'Thank you both for your understanding,' replied Mignemi. 'Shall I provide Alex with their details on the drive back to my apartment?'

'Yes, please do. And the arrangement can start immediately,' said Helmut.

They all shook hands and he left the room to find Alex waiting to take him home.

It had been a very eventful and tiring day and now he knew that he had just seven days to see how the cards would fall.

Chapter 27

Jimmy Skaa sat straddled over the lifeless body of Gary Jones. He was breathing hard. Not from the physical exertion of destroying the man's face with a Stanley knife but from the excitement he'd enjoyed whilst completing the deed. Molly's screaming had finally stopped and she sat leaning against the wall with her head bent forward. She was sobbing and she was terrified.

Skaa got to his feet, muttered something to himself, and walked up the steps out of the basement. He slumped onto the filthy settee picked up the remote and switched the television on. He stared at the screen oblivious to the droning voice of the woman recounting the local news stories of the day. In his mind, he replayed the events of the last hour. How Jones had riled him and forced him to get the gun and then shoot him. What might have happened if the shot had actually killed him? What would it have been like cutting up the face of a dead man? Would it have been as much fun? He recalled the ecstasy of cutting out the eyeballs and severing the optic nerve. All in all, it had been everything he'd hoped for and now that he was practised, the next time was likely to be even better!

He was snapped out this dream-like state when the screen flashed up a picture of a face he was sure he recognised. He turned up the sound and a huge grin broke out across his face. Well, would you believe it? There was a report on how the lovely Molly had gone missing and the police were asking if anyone had seen her. Next was a picture of the famous Justin Kell, brilliant! And it was all down to him. The news moved on to the next story but before he could settle back into his euphoria the *Voice* decided it was time for a reality check.

'Before you get too carried away there are certain matters that you need to consider. First off, you need to dispose of the body. Then there is young Molly to consider. If you are to use her as bait to get Kell here, then you need to formulate a plan and quickly. The fact that her disappearance is on the BBC news means it is just a matter of time before someone remembers seeing you with her outside the underground station and, if that happens, then it's just a matter of time before you get caught. Of course you might decide to have your fun with the girl and then move on and start again. In any event, you need an exit strategy if you want to avoid being caught.'

'Stop it, stop it! Why do you have to spoil my moment of glory! My triumph!'

'If you want to make a success of your new life as a serial killer, I suggest that you try and keep in the real world. You probably only have a week, two at the most to finish your work here and move on. If you don't, then it won't be a happy ending.'

'But my lists! I'm only just getting started.'

'The lists will keep. All you need to do is move on and make sure you don't leave any trace that it was you behind. You can move to another part of London and complete the work on all your stupid lists.'

He was about to argue that his lists weren't stupid, that they were in fact the work of a genius when the reality of the situation finally struck home. He stood up and went down to the basement leaving the television talking to itself.

'Now then, Molly my dear. I don't want you to be alarmed by what's happened here. You weren't actually meant to witness the demise of Mr Jones, but shit happens as the saying goes. I don't intend to harm you in the same way, providing that between us we can persuade your boss to come and visit without bringing any of his police friends with him. Now, how do you think we can do that?'

Molly stared at the lunatic standing above her and felt a glimmer of hope. If Justin were to come here then surely he'd be able to overpower the mad man and free her from the nightmare.

'Well, all I have to do is ring him or text him and ask him to come and get me. My phone is in my bag.'

'Mmmn, but what would be stopping him to come charging in here with half of the Met? No, I don't think that's the way at all Molly. I hope you're not trying to trick me?'

'Of course not. But if he's going to come here then he has to know where I am?'

'No, that's not the way. What I need to do is bring him here. If I can do that and not alert the police then I will be home and dry. Yes, that's what I need to do. I just have to make a new list and that will be that.'

Molly had heard him mention his lists on a couple of occasions and had determined it was just a part of the madness. But mad or not, she knew she had to keep on his good side to avoid being the target of one of his eruptions of violence.

'Yes, I agree that's the way to go. We don't want to involve the police that would just complicate things. Now I don't suppose I could have something to eat and drink, could I?'

He considered this question for a full thirty seconds, seeming to have a conversation with himself. Finally, he said: 'Yes, of course. I'll bring you something down in a minute or two.'

He turned and looked at the body on the other side of the room.

'Do you have any suggestions as to how I might dispose of Gary without drawing any attention to myself?'

Having studied all the sciences at A level, Molly was familiar with the use of various substances that were used to preserve organic material. It was also an area that was covered in her Criminology degree.

Despite the horror of the situation, Molly was in full survival mode, the adrenalin pumping round her body.

'Well, the first thing we need to do is put the body in a container of some sort. Preferably one that can be sealed. Then to preserve the body to slow decomposition I think the easiest thing to do is to cover it in lime.'

'Lime? What sort of lime and where do I get it from? A greengrocer?'

She put off her most patient voice, trying not to make him feel stupid.

'The type of lime I'm talking about is used a lot in building materials. You can get lime mortar or lime plaster for example. You can also get pure lime and mix it with water or weak acids depending on what you want to use it for.'

Skaa started howling with laughter and Molly wondered if she'd been too smart for her own good. Eventually, he got himself together. 'And I know just where I can get some! From Jones himself. He used to work at a builder's merchants you know. Oh, wouldn't that be so ironic? Burying the scum in some of his own lime!'

'Stop being ridiculous. There is no need to troop over to the other side of London just to get some lime mix. There are plenty of builders' yards here in Leytonstone that you can get it from without drawing undue attention to yourself. Now ask her how much you'll need and remember there's also the box to put him in to consider.'

She watched uneasily as Skaa had another conversation with himself.

'Now then Molly, what a good idea. How much do you think I'll need?'

She wasn't exactly sure but quickly decided this wouldn't be an answer he'd want to hear.

'I'd start by getting two large bags. If it's not enough we can always mix it with something like soil.'

She knew this sounded weak but on the other hand, she thought that by continually using "we" she might be able to gain a bit of rapport which would hopefully keep her alive until Justin came to rescue her.

'And as for the container, I suppose I could just order a coffin. After all, that's what it is, isn't it?' He started that ridiculous sniggering laugh that set her nerves right on edge.

'I think you could probably get something less conspicuous at the builder's yard which would save you time and no shopping around.'

'What an excellent idea. I'll go first thing in the morning. Now it's time we have our evening meal. Let me see what I can come up with.'

Molly checked her watch. It was seven-thirty in the evening and she was exhausted, hungry, and frightened. She had seen how easy Skaa's mood could swing and desperately hoped that she could keep on the right side of him. It was over an hour later that he returned with a tray holding two microwaved lasagne, a packet of biscuits, and cans of Coca-Cola.

'I thought that as we're getting on so well, we could eat together.'

He put the tray on the floor and passed her one of the microwaved meals.

'Yes, it's nice to have company, and thank you for such a lovely meal.'

They ate the food sitting on the floor without further conversation. All the time Molly was trying to think of something to say that might help her plan to escape. But the more she thought about it the more hopeless her situation seemed. Finally, she managed: 'Is there anything you need me to do to get Justin here?'

'No there isn't, thank you Molly. In the morning I'm going to get the lime and Gary's coffin.' Another snigger. 'Then, probably the day after I will go and see Mr Kell and ask him if he'd like to come for a visit.'

'That sounds like a great idea. If you wanted you could take a photo of me, just to prove that I'm here and I'm sure he'll want to come along straight away.'

Skaa turned his head slightly and gave her an inquisitive look as though she'd either said something very stupid or very clever.

'A photograph, yes that could be the answer. It could be just the incentive he needs. Now would you like a biscuit?' He opened the packet and passed it to her whilst talking to himself as usual.

Chapter 28

The next morning Skaa woke up feeling excited at the prospect of everything moving in the right direction. He opened up the Google app on his phone and typed in, "where can I buy lime". He scrolled through the array of responses which ranged from supermarkets that sold limes, a site promoting a credit card called lime, lime for the garden, what type of lime you can buy on Amazon...the list went on and on.

His immediate reaction was anger at Molly for trying to confuse him but as he stood up, the *Voice* of reason stepped in.

'Don't be surprised that there are all sorts of different types of lime. You just need to work through what exactly it is you need. I'm sure you'll find that it can be used for all sorts of things, so it would be sensible if you also had a story on what you want the lime for. After all, you can't say it's to stop a body you've got in your cellar decomposing and stinking the place out, can you?'

It took him nearly an hour to complete his research to the point where he was happy that he understood what the different types of lime were used for. His mind had concluded that what he needed was what he regarded as "proper lime", the sort you use to stop smells in outdoor toilets. He even had its chemical formula, CaO! He also discovered that people put lime on their lawns to make them grow better. He wasn't certain it was exactly the same type of lime but he reckoned it would be close enough. The *Voice* agreed, advising that it would also be easier to say that he wanted it for a lawn.

There was a retail park on the other side of town that had a B&Q, which stocked various types of lawn products and he was pretty certain he could get an appropriate container to put Jones' body in from there as well.

It took him half an hour to walk to the retail park and he headed straight to the garden section of the superstore. The shelves that stocked the various lawn products were stacked with an array of different treatments that left him bewildered as he scanned row after row of bags that would make your lawn greener and lusher than everyone else's.

'Can I help you, Sir? Are you looking for something for your lawn?'

He snapped around to see a smiling teenager beaming at him.

'Er, yes I am as a matter of fact. I'm looking for some lime.'

'We do have lime over here, Sir,' replied the youth as he walked to the far end of one of the rows. 'It is good on a lawn, but these products here are much better as they contain nitrogen, phosphorus, and potassium. Altogether a much better mix. They're a bit more expensive but well worth it.'

'But I just want lime. I've got to have lime. He told me I must get lime.'

The assistant took a step back and looked around to see if any of his colleagues were on hand. All of a sudden he had a very nervous feeling about the customer with the scarred face.

'Er, of course. Lime is also very good. How big is your lawn?'

'How big? I'm not sure. How big are the bags it comes in?'

'We only have one size, 25 kilograms.' The assistant was slowly moving away from the strange man, who now seemed to be having a conversation with himself.

'I think I better have…now let me see.' Skaa resumed his conversation with the *Voice* oblivious of the sales assistant who was staring at him with bug-eyed incredulity mixed with fear.

'I need to make sure I have enough and don't have to come back to this annoying store. So I'll take ten bags.'

As the strangest customer he had ever spoken to appeared to have returned to some semblance of normality, the assistant clicked back into helpful mode.

'I'll get them loaded on to a trolley and take them to the till for you. I can also help you load them into your car if you would like.'

'Car? But I don't have a car. How can you put them into a car if I don't have one?'

'Ah, so you would like to use our delivery service. That's fine but there will be a small charge as the cost does not meet the minimum for our free service.'

The assistant had moved a nearby flatbed trolley next to the shelves stacked with bags of hydrated lime and started to load them on one by one.

'It's far too risky to have them delivered. It will leave a trail. I suggest you abort this trip and just move quicker to secure Kell. The body may start to smell but providing you and the bitch can put up with it, who cares.'

'But if there is any delay, then the smell could also give me away. No, I'm going to continue. I'll pay with cash and that will be that.' It was unusual for Skaa to be so rational when having a debate with the *Voice* but this time he'd thought it through. Also when he'd had his fun with Kell and finally killed him, it would be sensible if he could also hide the smell of the decaying body for as long as possible.

As the teenage assistant was holding up a bag for the lady on the till to scan, Skaa said.

'Actually, if you can deliver, I'll take another ten bags. So twenty in all.' He smiled as he spoke as if he didn't have a care in the world.

The order of lime would be delivered that afternoon, between 3:00 pm and 5:00 pm. On his walk back, he went to the Army & Navy Surplus store and brought two single man tents. He hadn't forgotten about the list which had a container for a body on it but had decided he'd taken enough risks for one day by having the lime delivered. The tents were good quality and guaranteed waterproof. He would simply wrap Jones' body in the tent and fill it with lime. Genius!

The delivery driver knocked on the door and was relieved that he only had to dump the twenty 25 kg bags of lime on the pavement outside the front door. No steps to negotiate, no need to test his fragile back, and best of all from Skaa's perspective, he took no notice of what it was he was delivering.

Once he signed for the delivery, Skaa moved the bags into the front room and locked the front door. When he opened the door down to the cellar, he noticed the smell straight away. As he struggled down the steps with the first bag, he saw Molly huddled against the wall with her legs up against her chest. She didn't acknowledge him at all.

He dropped the bag of lime next to Jones' body. 'Molly, are you alright? What's the matter?'

'I thought you were my friend. I'm cold and hungry and it's started to stink down here and you don't even bring me any breakfast.' She didn't raise her voice. She just sounded like a sulking child.

'Oh, dear. I am sorry. It's just that I've been very busy today. But as soon as I've got these bags down here I'll get you a blanket and something to eat. How does that sound?'

'What about the smell? It's only going to get worse.'

'I'll sort that out as well. Just let me get Gary comfortable first.' He did that awful snigger as he went back upstairs to get the next bag.

He had clearly forgotten about the promise of a blanket and food as Molly watched the scar-faced maniac for the rest of the afternoon, bringing umpteen bags of hydrated lime down the steps and then placing the body in a small tent that had been laid flat on the floor. He then sliced open the bags one by one and started to pour the powder over the body. He'd got through about half of the bags when he turned towards her as if finally realising she was still there.

'I think I've misjudged the number of bags that I need. I thought ten would be enough for Gary and then I'd have ten left for your boss. But it seems like I'm going to need all of them for greedy Gary.' Snigger.

'What about the food you promised me and the blanket?' Molly raised her voice but didn't shout.

'Well, I've nearly finished here, so I'll make us tea in a few minutes and we can have some biscuits as well. How does that sound?'

'You certainly know how to spoil a lady.'

He ignored the remark and carried on slitting open the bags and pouring the powdery pellets over the body. When all the bags were empty, he stood back to admire his work. Most of the body was covered but even with twenty bags some of the extremities were still showing. Anyway, it will have to be enough he thought, it's only ex-con Gary Jones after all.

He zipped up the tent and then rolled the remaining canvas around the body. When this was complete he continued to roll the body into the far corner. He was pleasantly surprised that hardly any of the lime had spilled out of the makeshift shroud. He proceeded to get the tent material as tight as he could around the body and then used the guy ropes to secure it.

'There! I think you'll agree that I've done a very good job. Let's hope that keeps the smell at bay. Now it's time for tea.'

Skaa was still covered in the dust from the bags of lime when he returned ten minutes later with two cups of tea and the remains of yesterday's biscuits. Molly gratefully slurped her tea and started to gobble down the biscuits.

'Don't forget the photograph. You need to send it to him today. Take it on her phone and go into the city and text him from somewhere else. I think they can trace where phones are when you send texts. Make it dramatic and then you can meet him and get him to come here.'

'Okay, I understand. Now then Molly what do you think about this photograph? Which is your better side?'

'My backside is probably my best look at the moment.'

Molly saw the red mist start to descend and regretted what she thought was quite an amusing retort.

'Oh my, that is funny. Quite the comedienne, aren't you? How about I stick my gun right up your best backside and blow you inside out!' He stood and was towering over her shouting as loud as he could.

'Sorry, I'm so sorry. I didn't mean it. I was just trying to be funny.'

Skaa turned around and went up the cellar steps. Seconds later he returned with the gun. He stood over the whimpering woman and slowly raised the weapon until it was pointing at her head. 'Do you think you're funny now, Molly?' He turned his head to give that inquisitive look she hated as much as his stupid sniggers.

She looked up defiantly. 'No, I'm not the funny one, you pathetic little man. You are. You think you're big and brave but just you wait till Justin gets here. He'll show you what a real man is really like.'

She didn't notice any reaction in his face, but she did see him slowly start to pull the trigger.

She shut her eyes and waited for oblivion. When she only heard a click followed by a grating snigger she didn't know if she was relieved or not.

'It's not loaded. I took all the bullets out as a precaution. It's a good job I did, isn't it Molly? Otherwise, your brains, that is if you've got any brains, would be splattered all over the cellar. And I haven't got any lime left to stop you smelling! Now let's take this photograph and get it over to Mr soon to be dead Kell.'

Molly was shaking as the mad man who was getting more unstable by the minute pulled her to her feet and got her standing with her back to the wall. Then he got the gun and tried to get her to hold the barrel in her mouth. He got frustrated when he realised it was too heavy for her to hold for more than second, so he got her to spread her arms like a crucifix and place the gun in her right hand so it was pointing at her head. He took her phone and held his thumb on the screen for five seconds. He didn't realise that he'd taken twenty-eight images in rapid succession but was delighted with the results. The lighting was poor but this only enhanced the terror in the eyes of a bedraggled and terrified young woman, held in shackles in a dingy cellar pointing a gun at her own head. Yes, he was very, very pleased with the results.

Chapter 29

Amy watched as Justin mooched around the apartment they were viewing. She knew he was going through the motions and had other more important things on his mind, but she'd hoped a day of trekking around available apartments with stunning views across the river would take his mind off Molly, if only for a few hours.

'What do you think?' she asked.

'It's very nice and the location is great. The second bedroom is a bit small but it would be okay to put a desk in for a home office.' He was desperately trying to be enthusiastic about actually buying their first home together but his mind couldn't escape from Molly's disappearance. It had been 72 hours and he knew that the longer the clock kept ticking the less likely it was that she'd be found alive.

'Come on, let's go and get something to eat and have a chat about which we ones we like. I've already had a couple of the agents texting me asking if we'll be putting in an offer.' She put her arms around his neck, pulled him towards her, and gently kissed his lips. 'I know you've got a lot on your mind, but its Sunday. Let's enjoy what's left of the weekend and hope they find Molly soon.'

'Yeah, you're right. My fretting about everything isn't going to do any good.'

'And stop checking your phone every two minutes. You'll hear it if it rings or a text comes in.'

The agent was waiting for them in the small hallway that entered the apartment. 'Do you like it?'

'It's very nice,' replied Amy. 'The second bedroom is a bit small but we could turn into an office. We've seen five properties over the weekend so we're going to take a bit of time to think it over and we'll let you know next week.'

They both thanked him for showing them around and headed for an Italian restaurant that Amy had been to a couple of times. 'With a bit of luck, we'll get a table on the terrace. It's only five o'clock, so we should be okay.'

The restaurant was very busy. It was a lovely warm June day in London and every table on the terrace was occupied. The waiter suggested that if they had a drink at the bar then a table would be free in about twenty minutes.

It was well worth the wait. The table was on the far side of the patio with an unobstructed view up and down the river. Once they ordered their food and a bottle of Sauvignon Blanc Amy got out her iPad and starting talking through the pros and cons of the various properties they'd seen. Justin finally managed to push all thoughts of Molly out of his mind and by the time they'd finished their meal they'd got it down to a choice of two.

'Okay, that's good progress. I'll make appointments for a second viewing on these two. What nights would be good for you next week?'

As he got his phone out to check his diary, it rang. It gave him a start when he saw it was Packham's mobile.

'Chris, have you found her?'

'Sorry Justin, no we haven't. But I do have some disturbing news on the Llubovs.'

There was a slight pause before Kell said: 'Don't tell me, they've escaped!'

'Got it in one. Look there's a bit more to it than them just escaping. Can I come to your office first thing in the morning? There's something that doesn't feel at all right about this mess and I've got a couple of ideas I'd like to blow by you. Can you make it for 7:30, then I can get into the madhouse by nine?'

'Sure, 7:30 is fine. See you then.'

The second he clicked off the call Amy said rather harshly: 'I hope that's not 7:30 this evening.'

'No, it's in the morning. But if it was this evening would it matter? I've got a lot going on at the moment Amy. I thought you understood.'

She softened her tone slightly: 'I do understand, of course, I do. Is it news about Molly?'

'Er no, it's about the Llubovs. They've escaped.'

Amy just stared at him, her mind slamming through the implications of what she'd just heard. Despite the possibility that it could mean that her life was in danger, she came out with: 'You promised me that you wouldn't have any more involvement in all that stuff Justin. It's gone, it's history. You promised me you would move on and stop torturing yourself. You lied to me!'

'But Amy…'

He didn't get the chance to finish his sentence. She stood up and stormed across the patio with every head turning to watch her go.

The next morning Packham was waiting outside his friend's office and watched as he walked down Brick Lane just before 7:30.

'Christ Justin, you look rough. Heavy night was it?'

'And good morning to you too.'

He trudged up the stairs, opened the office, and put the kettle on. When they both had a cup of strong black coffee, he recounted how it was his friend's call that had resulted in a long difficult evening trying to explain to Amy that he wasn't actively involved in the aftermath of the Horizon scandal.

'But you haven't actually been involved since we met that Smithe guy. Do you want me to talk to her?'

'No, thanks. I think there's a bit more to it than that. I can't get Molly out of my mind. I feel I'm responsible in some way and I think Amy resents that there's this other woman sucking all the energy and emotion out of me.'

'That doesn't sound like Amy. Are you sure that's all it is?'

'Well, she's pushing for us to buy a fancy apartment together. She's moving our relationship on at a pace that I'm uncomfortable with. It's probably just the stress of everything that's going on at the moment. I'm sure we'll work it out. Anyway, tell me how the Llubovs managed to escape your clutches. I thought they had these implants that tracked their every move?'

'They did.'

Packham recounted the timeline and details of the escape.

Kell listened intently, making notes as Packham described the perfect operation.

'Very clever.' said Kell. 'So clearly Santini gave them the heads up that that operation was "go" and then just disappeared so he can say he had nothing to do with it. I assume that our friend Andrei took something to make him fit?'

'From what eyewitnesses say, it certainly wasn't an act. We suspect Santini provided whatever it was. There was no trace of anything in the food and drink either of them had. The fake ambulance was clearly waiting close by and they knew they would be on the scene before the proper one arrived. It was military precision in the planning.'

Kell picked up the thought process: 'They remove the implants in the ambulance and pass them to an accomplice who drives to the hospital and dumps them in a bin outside. Brilliant.'

'They even put the individual trackers in a special tube so there were about three feet apart. So even the signal looked realistic.' Packham shook his head as he spoke in admiring disbelief.

He went on: 'We're satisfied our surveillance guy is not involved. He made a few fundamental mistakes but that's what they were, mistakes. Being in front of the ambulance was a schoolboy error, as was letting a vehicle come in between them.'

'Was this vehicle part of the escape?' asked Kell.

Packham laughed: 'No. It was a Mr Patrick O'Shaunessy driving his wife to A&E after she poured boiling water over her hand making a pot of tea. So they even had the luck of the Irish on their side.'

They sat in silence while they finished their drinks.

Then the policeman said: 'We also lost track of Mignemi for most of that day as well.'

Again Kell just listened as his friend told how they had seen Mignemi into his flat the previous afternoon but then nothing for the rest of the following day until he appeared walking down Chiltern Street in the evening.

'He told us he'd been for a walk in Regents Park and then spent the rest of the day at the British Library. He apparently left by the staff entrance at the back of the apartment block. We've reviewed all the CCTV footage and there's no sign of him on any of them.'

'So, what's your next move? Are you going to bring him in for more questioning?'

'The powers that be are having a pissing contest over what happens next. In reality, we can't charge him with anything. He's done nothing wrong and there's not even any circumstantial evidence. The spooks want to take him off the streets and make him disappear. Just end the problem. But you can imagine that the politically correct brigade is appalled at even the suggestion.'

Kell started flipping through his notebook, going back and forth between various pages of scrawled notes.

Packham sat watching in anticipation of some brilliant Holmes type piece of deduction. And he wasn't disappointed.

'I know how Mignemi got out of his apartment without being seen.' Kell looked at the policeman and gave him a rueful grin.

He continued: 'I'm surprised the combined brains of the Metropolitan Police and the security services haven't figured it out.'

'Damn, what have we missed that only the great Justin Kell has spotted?'

'Instead of checking the CCTV footage between the staff entrance, Regents Park and the British Library, I think if you look at the exit to the car park under the apartment block and the route across the city to Bermondsey, you'll see a very normal looking ambulance taking great care not to attract any undue attention. It won't be enough for the CPS to move on but you can certainly rattle our friend Alfio's cage.'

Packham just shook his head. 'You'll be right of course. As usual, this is going to make us all look stupid.'

Kell smiled: 'I think you can come out of this quite well. After all, you'll be the one who makes the connection. A feather in the cap of the Met and one in the eye for the spooks.'

'I guess you're right. Anyway, I best get into work with my case breaking lead. Thanks, Justin.'

As he stood to leave Kell said: 'One more thing. If they've gone to all this trouble to break out a couple of their thugs, then I suspect something else is about to go down. Something big. This is why I'd focus on Mignemi. Oh, and one more thing, send me an update on Molly and tell them I want to be involved.'

'Will do, and thanks again, Justin.'

Chapter 30

Mignemi could not be certain that Alex and his friends were no longer watching his every move. He was however sure that the UK authorities would be. Despite this, it was still relatively straight forward to leave his apartment without being spotted. If he was, then the underground was the ideal place to lose a tail.

It was Monday morning so the plethora of commuters was at its peak when he made his way to the Baker Street tube station. This time he did leave by the staff entrance and once he'd weaved his way through to the station, visiting various of the platforms, he was satisfied that no one was following.

He got the Metropolitan line to Liverpool Street and then the Stanstead Express out to the airport. He got in the taxi at the back of the line which then made its circuitous route to the farmhouse.

Santini was waiting for him in the courtyard and ushered him into the kitchen where the Llubovs and Hendrick were waiting.

The greetings were completed quickly and Mignemi commenced the briefing.

'I have been accepted by the Aljadid leaders into their ranks. They verified the information I previously delivered and want to proceed immediately with the destruction of the Maktab. I have advised them that the next meeting will be a week on Thursday.'

Santini spoke: 'Did they accept the bullshit about the meetings following the cycle of the moon?'

Mignemi smiled: 'Yes they did. No questions asked.'

He turned to the siblings and Hendrick. 'They are happy for me to have my own driver. Hendrick that will be you. I am also allowed to provide my own security, Andrei and Darya, of course.

Tomorrow Hendrick will drive us to their headquarters in Holland Park. There is an underground car park that has two security staff at the entrance and a further one at the door to the stairwell which contains the lift. Hendrick, you will be responsible for taking care of these three guards. The visit tomorrow should be sufficient time for you to prepare. Andrei, Darya—you will escort me up to the second floor. This is the top floor of the building where their meetings take place. You will be required to wait on the corridor outside of the meeting with the other security staff. I am uncertain of the number but we can check tomorrow. My guess is there will be five. Any questions?'

'How long will the meeting last?' asked Hendrick.

'I am only there to deliver the briefing to enable their attack on the Maktab. I expect it to be no more than an hour. They will request that I leave once the briefing has been completed and I have answered their questions.'

'When do we take them out?' This time it was Darya who asked the question.

'I will recommend that the meeting reconvenes on the night of their assault. The time difference is such that it will be midday here in the UK. I will suggest that I attend that meeting and it is then that we will destroy them. Miguel, is the briefcase ready?'

Santini put a hard aluminium briefcase on the table. 'It is all prepared with the false bottom. You can take it tomorrow for the briefing packs. Hendrick will fill it with the explosive for the following week.'

Hendrick nodded his agreement. 'How will you get to leave the briefcase and get yourself out without being blown up?'

'It will be a simple trip to the lavatory. I will detonate the bomb and Andrei and Darya will take care of the guards. You will have secured our exit by removing the security in the garage.'

Santini stood up. 'Very good Alfio. The best plans are the straight forward ones. I am returning to Beirut this afternoon and will be there to witness the trap of the would-be assassins. Good luck to you all.'

Mignemi waited until the solicitor had left before asking if there were any further questions. When no one spoke he said: 'Right then, Hendrick if you can drive me back to London and we can discuss the timings for tomorrow.'

As the car pulled away, Mignemi asked the driver: 'What is the matter with Andrei? He doesn't speak at all. No questions, no comments. Is he in the right frame of mind for the operation?'

'He's annoyed with the poisoning in the café. He thinks it was reckless and not needed. He keeps saying that he could have been killed.'

'Does he say this to Santini?'

'No, just to me and his sister. I think he has lost his trust in us.'

Mignemi didn't say anything further. But he wondered what the effect would be on the three of them when they realised the full extent of his plan.

'You can drop me by Kings Cross and I'll walk the rest of the way. We need to be in Holland Park at 10:00 pm tomorrow, so I will meet you in the car park of my building at 9:00. This will give us plenty of time.'

As he strolled down Euston Road in the early evening sunshine, he pondered on the timing of contacting Detective Inspector Packham. He couldn't risk being apprehended and held by the authorities at this stage of the operation, and it was important he gave the authorities as small amount of time as possible to interfere with his plan.

When he entered the underground garage the following evening, he saw two Audi Q7's with blacked-out rear windows. He smiled as Hendrick got out of one and opened the door for him.

'I thought it might help if the car park is being watched. They won't know which one to follow.' said the young man.

'You are very thorough, thank you.' replied Mignemi.

The two identical cars turned in different directions when they emerged from the car park on Chiltern Street. If the police were following they'd have to make a choice of which way to go.

'Keep an eye for a tail please, Hendrick. I'm not overly concerned if they see where we are going but I don't want the security services to spook our target. Andrei, are you alright? You haven't spoken a word in any of our meetings.'

'I'm fine Alfio. I'm still getting my head around my poisoning, but I'm focused on what needs doing.'

'Very good. Tonight you just make friends. Take it easy. Gain their trust. Next week you can have your fun.'

They drove in silence the rest of the way.

The two guards at the entrance to the garage checked their identities but didn't search the car. Similarly, the man at the entrance to the lobby just welcomed them and showed them into the lift.

The brother and sister escorted Mignemi down the corridor where the security for the Al Khamsa was waiting. He had been correct, there were five of them. At exactly 10:00 pm the door opened and he entered the room to see the familiar faces of Irini and Helmut plus two further men and one woman. He put them all at a similar age, maybe early forties. Irini did the introductions. Mignemi opened his briefcase and pulled out six folders that were handed around the table.

'Firstly, I must inform you that the date of the meeting of the Maktab has changed. It will be one week from today. The reason being there is a large arms shipment coming into the port and they are finalising the terms of the deal with the Russians.'

'This breaks the routine that you told us of Alfio? Are you certain?' asked Irini.

'Yes, I am certain. All of the Maktab will be present. They will assemble in one of the warehouses adjacent to the wharf. They will conclude the terms for the shipment and finalise the distribution of the weapons. It is not unusual for such a change to be made.'

'Very well, continue.' said Irini.

The details of the location are shown here. He held up a piece of A3 paper that resembled an ordnance survey map. The Qadim controls the wharf and there is only one road in and out. It is always guarded by four soldiers armed with automatic weapons. The perimeter around the warehouse will also be guarded by four soldiers, one at each corner. The Maktab's individual security will be with them in the warehouse. All the details are in your folders.

'So how do you propose we achieve our objective?' It was Helmut this time who asked the question.

'I have arranged for a boat to be at the far end of the harbour, in the dock area. You will be able to load sufficient artillery onto the boat and then it's simply a case of blowing up the warehouse from the water and escaping up the coast. Again, all the details are in your folders. I have a man loyal to me, to captain the boat and two crew members. If you prefer, I am happy for you to provide the captain and crew.'

He paused and looked around and saw the three men and two women studying the documents and nodding. The attack must take place at 2:00 pm local time, midday here in London. There is also the opportunity to secure the cache of weaponry, but that is outside of my remit and is likely to be a more difficult task.'

Again he paused and looked around the table. No questions just nodding.

'I would like to suggest we all meet at the time of the attack and when you get confirmation of its success, you will accept my worth to join you. I will also be in a position by then to bring you full details of the Qadim network, including the cells throughout Europe and Asia and their hierarchies.'

He sat down and waited for the objections to be raised.

'It seems almost too easy Alfio. Are you sure this will work?' asked Helmut.

'I am certain. The best plan is the simplest one. One direct hit with a hand-held mortar will be sufficient to destroy the warehouse. As you will see I suggest that you hit it up to six times just be on the safe side.' He smiled his most confident smile.

'Excellent, thank you, Alfio. We will finalise the arrangements and meet again on Tuesday at 11:45. Thank you again. You may leave us.' Irini nodded and he put his folder back in his briefcase and left the room.

In the corridor, Darya was joking with one the guards with Andrei standing stock-still as though on sentry duty.

When they reached the car park, Hendrick was in discussion with the guard outside the stairwell, but quickly moved to open the car door for his boss when he came out of the lift.

Hendrick waved to the two men at the entrance as they headed out into the night.

'Did anyone have any problems?' asked Mignemi.

'Not me, it all went like clockwork,' replied Hendrick.

'No problems,' said the siblings in unison.

'Very good, everything is on track.'

They drove back to the city in silence, leaving Mignemi to ponder his next move, particularly when to have a conversation with the policeman and also Justin Kell.

Back in Holland Park, the five leaders of the Aljadid finished reading the dossiers their potential new recruit had supplied.

'The information is comprehensive and the level of detail gives it credibility,' said Irini.

Helmut responded: 'Yes, indeed. But I do not like the idea that the boat is not crewed by our men. I suggest that we neutralise the crew and proceed with just our own forces. That way we can be certain of success. And what of our new found friend and ally Mr Mignemi? You are not seriously proposing that he join our rank in any capacity, are you?'

'Of course not. When he returns next week and we get the confirmation of the destruction of our enemy we will kill him. He is an old man of little value to us. We will proclaim his death as the final acclamation that the old is gone and that we are the new power in the world.' Irini closed her folder and stood up. The meeting was over.

Chapter 31

Skaa had been studying the photographs he'd taken of his hostage for half an hour and still couldn't decide which one to send to Kell. The fact that he didn't appreciate that all twenty-eight of them were virtually identical made the task just that little bit harder. In the end, he plumped for the first one in the sequence.

'I suggest you make sure you understand how that phone operates and how you attach a photograph to a text. You don't want to get all the way into town and then realise you can't work it.'

This was the first time the *Voice* had spoken to him for some time and it momentarily jolted him further into his insanity.

He spoke aloud, 'What do you want? I know perfectly well how to operate a phone. Now leave me alone I've got work to do.'

'Just make sure you have it all planned out. Sending Kell the message is one thing but dealing with him when he gets here is another matter altogether, especially if he brings someone else with him.'

'But he won't risk that if he wants to see his precious Molly alive. Anyway, I've already thought that through. I'm not going to be in when he gets here. I'll be around the corner and will surprise him with a tap of a lump hammer.' He paused before saying; 'So there!'

'Very good. And when are you going to put the plan into operation? It's Sunday morning, so is it better to do it now when everywhere is quiet or on a weekday when there are more people around? Is morning, afternoon, or evening better? Have you thought these things through?'

'Yes, I have actually. I'm going to strike on Tuesday. I've decided the early afternoon will be best and that gives me Monday to review all my lists. I will go to his office first and make sure he's inside. Then I will send him the picture and tell him to go immediately to Liverpool Street and get the Central Line to Leytonstone. I will follow him and make sure no police are involved and then I'll text him again when he gets out of the station with the address. I'll follow him and when he's outside I smack him in the head with the hammer and that will be that! See, I told you I didn't need your help.'

When the *Voice* did not respond, he turned his attention back to Molly's phone and decided he should check with her how to send the picture to Kell.

Molly looked up when she heard the door at the top of the steps open and saw her jailer with a bottle of diet cola and what looked like a sandwich. She couldn't remember the last time she ate anything and started salivating at the thought of food and a sweet drink.

'Now then Molly, it's time for some lunch. I've got you a nice cheese sandwich and a bottle of diet cola. I decided you are the type of girl who likes a diet drink. No sugary fat that's going to ruin your figure.'

He put the two items on the floor, took a step back, and looked down waiting for her response.

'Thank you, I do like cheese and diet drinks, you must be very perceptive.'

As she unwrapped the sandwich and started to wolf it down, Skaa puffed his chest out at the compliment. He waited until she'd finished eating and had gulped down half of the drink before he spoke.

'You'll be pleased to know that you'll have some company in a couple of days. I'm going to send our Mr Kell your photograph and invite him to come for a visit.' He sniggered his annoying snigger that made her feel like someone was pulling their fingernails down a blackboard. She managed to smile but didn't say anything.

'But first I want you to show me how you attach a picture to a text.' He pulled the phone out of his pocket, took a step towards her, squatted down on his haunches, and handed her the phone.

'It's better if you send it by WhatsApp. Here I'll show you.'

She turned the phone so they could both see the screen.

'This is the WhatsApp icon.' She pointed to the green icon on the screen with the white telephone inside a text bubble with a left-pointing tail. She touched it and the screen showed various groups and individuals with whom she had recently chatted with.

Skaa stared at the screen as if spellbound.

She closed the screen and said. 'Now the first thing is to decide which picture you want to send.' She touched the Photos icon and the screen showed multiple images of her holding the gun to her own head.

'You simply tap on the picture you want to send,' she picked a random one of the twenty-eight which filled the screen. 'Next, you tap on the square with an arrow pointing upwards and then you'll see the WhatsApp icon. You then just tap on the icon and decide who you want to send it to.'

Finally, he broke out of his trance-like state and said: 'I can't see Kell's name.'

'That's because I haven't contacted him recently. All you do is scroll down until you see his name and then tap it, like this. Then you tap the next button here, in the bottom right-hand corner, and as you can see, there's the picture. You can type whatever you want in the Add a caption, section and then simply press the blue arrow and bingo, the picture and your message is sent.'

She knew there was no signal in the basement and had decided not to antagonise the mad man in case she ended up getting shot. The only way that she was going to get out of this was if Justin came to her rescue.

He got her to show him the process over and over until he was finally satisfied he understood it fully. Finally, he stood up and walked back up the steps without saying another word.

That night he agonised over his plan debating with himself as to whether the quiet of mid-afternoon or the chaos of the rush hour would be best for getting Kell to come rushing to Molly's rescue. After much deliberation he decided to stick with Tuesday afternoon. The more people that were around the more that could go wrong and he didn't want anything or anyone interfering at this stage. He would arrive early afternoon and then ring his quarry, making it very clear what would happen to little Miss Molly if he didn't follow his instructions to the letter.

It was warm and sunny as he arrived outside Kell's office. He checked the time on his and Molly's phone and was delighted when they both showed the same time, 13.39 He decided to use his own burner phone to make the call and then send the picture with its added message with Molly's. He spent most of last night deciding on exactly how to phrase what he wanted to say and had memorised it to avoid having to write it down.

He knew the *Voice* was right so slowly walked up and down Brick Lane trying to compose himself thinking about how many items he'd be able to tick off his numerous lists in a 'couple of hours' time.

Lost in his own deranged world, it was half an hour later when he found himself back outside Kell's office. Perfect! He got out his phone and dialled the number he wanted from memory.

Chapter 32

It was Sunday evening and Mignemi sat in his apartment contemplating the plan he had formulated and his motives behind it. He had settled on the fact that the plan, if not flawless was the best that had a higher than average chance of success. That was the easy part. His motives behind what he intended to play out sat less comfortably with him. It wasn't that he no longer had ambitions and dreams. His work was his life and he knew that if he didn't take matters into his own hands and take decisive action then at best he would be killed and at worst become a lackey for a second rate organised crime gang.

His father had always told him that when faced with a dilemma make a decision, be decisive. Don't just do nothing and hope the problem will go away or mend itself; you have to take matters into your own hands.

He had no time for the Aljadid and their so-called Al Khamsa. He despised them for what they were. Jumped up thugs, only recently out of nappies who were trying to play in the big league. They deserved their fate and he would be the one to administer it on Tuesday. What he was still trying to rationalise himself was his betrayal of the Maktab. They too would be wiped out in the same operation. The one they had given to him so he could prove his loyalty and save his own soul. Changing the date of the Aljadid attack meant they would all be there in the Beirut warehouse, cosying up to their new-found Russian friends. With luck and god willing they would be destroyed and he would step into their shoes and take over the Qadim.

He thought back to the numerous times he'd told his story to the Aljadid. Of how he felt betrayed by them, how they did not respect the lifelong service he had given them, how they were seemingly testing his loyalty with a task that could be carried out by any competent junior officer. They had belittled him and it had hurt.

There had been rumours he was going to be the first new blood to be appointed to the Maktab since it formed back in 1979. The original thirteen were now just seven and if he were not planning to end their lives, albeit only slightly prematurely, what would happen in the next few years when they simply died-off one by one?

He sipped his brandy and tried to settle his mind. The decision was made. He would be decisive and take control of his own destiny.

As with all plans, there were always variables that could not be fully controlled. In this case, there were two. Firstly, how would Santini react? The fact that he had returned to Beirut made his plans here more straightforward. The change of date for the strike would not be challenged by his three comrades. But what if Santini was at the warehouse for some reason? It would be unusual as he was always kept well away from front line operations. But what if? Assuming he wasn't, then his plan was to ring him as soon as was possible after the attack. If all went to plan, Al Khamsa and the Maktab would be gone and they would need to move quickly to make sure no one else filed the vacuum. That his friend was in Beirut would help, but how he would react? Well, he would just have to wait and see.

The other variable was which of the three who were now tied to his fate should he trust? He had made that decision earlier in the day when he made the call and asked them to meet him here at the apartment this evening. He checked his watch which showed 19:28 and one minute later the intercom buzzed.

He welcomed Hendrick and they sat at the modest-sized table in the kitchen/diner section of the apartment. He poured him a glass of water while he topped up his brandy.

'Thank you for coming and for being so punctual. I assume you were not followed?'

'I left the car at the airport and came in by train. I arrived about an hour ago and can confirm no one is watching the building.'

'How can you be so sure?'

Hendrick shrugged his shoulders as if to say, "*are you serious*", but was more considered in his response to his superior. 'I was trained by the best. I do not make mistakes. I am certain, one hundred per cent.'

Mignemi smiled: 'Excellent. I knew I'd made the right choice.'

Hendrick knew better than to ask the obvious question, so just sat there with a neutral look on his face.

Finally, Mignemi sighed, put his drink down, and started to stroll about the room. 'We live in difficult times, my young friend. The world is changing and not for the better. We are mere pawns on the chessboard, being moved about by others, sacrificed where needs be to help them win their petty game. I have always been a believer in taking matters into my own hands when an opportunity presents itself and the time is right. Instead of being a pawn, becoming the player. Taking control and moving the pieces as they should and must be moved.'

He paused to look at the young man sitting at the table. He saw no reaction, just the same neutral look on his face.

'The opportunity that now presents itself involves moving the destruction of Al Khamsa forward by two days, to Tuesday. The time is the same just the day has changed. So I need the briefcase to be fully prepared. I assume this doesn't cause an issue?'

'Not at all Alfio, I have everything ready. Why has the meeting been pulled forward?'

He'd considered at length whether full disclosure was the best policy and decided against it. He liked Hendrick, liked his calm self-assurance and professionalism, but it was too early to take him fully into his confidence.

'Quite simply, there is no need to wait. It also coincides with other matters that are taking place in Beirut, but they are not our concern. It is, however, important that we keep the new timeline to just the four of us, and then only telling Andrei and Darya at the last possible moment. I suggest that you advise them that I want a further briefing here in the city on Tuesday and then only inform them of the change when they are in the car.'

'I'm not sure Andrei will appreciate being kept in the dark. He's moody enough as it is. It feels like he's on the verge of exploding, lashing out, potentially doing something stupid.'

He had considered the male sibling's emotional state and decided it was something that could be managed. After all, he would soon get the opportunity to vent his anger by killing the Al Khamsa guards. But Hendrick was right, if Andrei reacted badly to being kept in the dark, especially when Hendrick had the inside track, then the whole operation could be put at risk.

Make a decision, be decisive. 'Very well. When you get back this evening, inform them of the change of plan. As you are the driver and do not have a *most wanted* poster following you around, that is the reason that I chose to brief you in person. It is also true to say that I do not trust everyone in our organisation right now and am therefore avoiding phone contact wherever possible. This will hopefully keep him calm long enough to fulfil his duty on Tuesday.'

Hendrick nodded in agreement. 'Is there anything else?'

'No, thank you, Hendrick. Have a safe trip back to the farmhouse and I will see you on Tuesday morning.'

When the door shut behind the man he was putting his trust in, he sat back in the armchair he favoured and continued to sip his drink. There was just one more task to complete in his preparation but that would have to wait until the morning.

The next day dawned bright and sunny and the views of the London skyline were are beautiful as ever. He showered, dressed, and ate a small breakfast of fruit and muesli accompanied by his usual coffee. When his watch showed 9:00 am, he dialled the main switchboard at the Metropolitan Police Headquarters and asked for DI Packham.

There were no formalities of asking who was calling and the next thing the voice at the other end of the line said: 'DI Packham.'

'Mr Packham, it is Alfio Mignemi. How are you on this beautiful morning?'

'Very well, thank you. What can I do for you Alfio? Are you ringing to confess your sins?'

'Not at all. But I do have some information that I think you'll find both interesting and useful. I would like to meet privately with you and also your friend Mr Kell if that is possible. What I have to say cannot be said over the phone. Oh, and it has to be today.'

The line was quiet for a moment while Packham considered the out-of-the-blue request.

'Okay, I suggest we meet at Justin's office on Brick Lane, say 4:30? It's private and we won't be seen. Do you know where it is?'

'I'm sure I can find it Mr Packham, 4:30 it is.' And with that, he ended the call.

Packham rang his friend who picked up immediately.

'Is it about Molly? Have you found her?'

'Sorry Justin, no it's not. But I have just had a very strange call from our friend Alfio. He wants to meet us both this afternoon and I suggested your office at 4:30. So whatever you've got planned, change it.'

'Bloody hell! Amy's going to kill me. We've got a second viewing on an apartment at 5:00. She's really keen on it and we'll almost certainly put in an offer. She'll be so mad.'

'He specifically asked that you be there Justin, so square it away with Amy and I'll see you at 4:30.'

Packham ended the call leaving Kell with a sinking feeling that his personal life was about to take a significant downturn. He rang her mobile and wasn't surprised when it went straight to voicemail. He left a message saying something very important had come up and that she would have to do the viewing on her own. He asked her to call him so he could explain what was happening and that if she was sure that the apartment was right for them then to go ahead and put in the offer they agreed.

He wasn't surprised when she didn't call back and they didn't speak again until it was way too late to explain what had happened.

At 4:30 on the dot, the intercom buzzed and Kell pressed the button that opened the door to the street. He went out onto the landing and watched Mignemi climb the stairs.

'Good afternoon, Mr Kell.'

'Good afternoon, Alfio. I'd say it's a pleasure to see you again, but it isn't.'

As he showed his visitor into the office the intercom buzzed again and he let the policeman in.

Kell was not inclined to offer his guest tea or coffee, but as Packham went over to the kitchen unit and put the kettle on he felt obliged to do so. When they had their drinks, Packham simply said: 'Well?'

'I have significant information about an event tomorrow that will be of great interest to you Mr Packham as it will change the face of organised crime here in London. Depending on how you use this information you may even become a hero or get that promotion you feel you should have had.'

'I'm not interested in being a hero, or a promotion for that matter, but I am interested in what you have to say.'

'Of course, forgive me. I'm aware of how altruistic you English people can be. Anyway, tomorrow afternoon the so-called leadership of the Aljadid, they call themselves Al Khamsa will be destroyed. All will be killed by a rival operation.'

'And we all know who that is, don't we Alfio?' said Packham.

Mignemi ignored the interruption and continued. 'At the same time, the Maktab will also be destroyed. If both events happen as I expect they will, then there will be a vacuum in the control of these organisations that you and I can both take advantage of.'

Packham grinned but managed not to laugh: 'And how would that be Alfio? How can we both benefit from such fortuitous events?'

'I intend to take control of the Qadim network. I will destroy what remains of Aljadid and will cease all Qadim operations here in London. This will leave you with just the Russians and Albanians to worry about, but it will be seen as a significant breakthrough against organised crime.'

Packham and Kell said nothing, waiting to see if he had finished. He had not.

'For this, I want safe passage out of your country. Technically, there is no reason why I can't simply board a plane and fly anywhere I want. But I am not stupid and understand that some of your colleagues in the security services may have a different view on what they would like to happen with me.'

Kell finally spoke: 'What about the Llubovs? We know you must have been involved in their escape. We want them to face justice.'

He had been expecting this question and so played what he hoped would be his trump card.

'When I have news that the events I mention have been satisfactorily completed, I will call in here and provide you with the address where you can find the Llubovs. This is, of course, subject to you ensuring my freedom to leave the country.'

'You haven't left me with much time to put these arrangements in place.' said Packham.

'Exactly. I expect to be here at around 2.00pm tomorrow, maybe a touch earlier. I will see you gentlemen then.'

As he stood to leave, Kell asked: 'Why was it so important that I was here at this meeting?'

'Ah yes, I almost forgot. I wanted to tell you to your face that my former masters instructed me to kill you Mr Kell. That was part of their terms to let me live. I will not be completing that task and when you pick up the Llubovs that danger is also removed. Again, a sign of good faith. I will see you gentlemen tomorrow.' And with that, he left.

Kell and Packham looked at each other, stunned into silence. Eventually, Kell said: 'Aren't I the lucky one? What do you think? Is he genuine or are we being played?'

'Oh, I think he's genuine alright and this might just get me that promotion I definitely do deserve. Now, I must get back to the madhouse and position this just right. Then it's just a case of waiting until tomorrow.'

Packham got a patrol car to get him back to the station. On the way, he radioed ahead to set up a briefing with the DCI. At this stage he didn't want to involve the interested parties in the Security Services as that would certainly take things out of the Met's hands and that just wasn't going to happen.

Chapter 33

The wrath of Amy's voicemail, when he'd not made the apartment viewing was so intense that he decided to have a few drinks and spend the night in the Premier Inn Hub across the road. She'd been close to hysteria calling him all sort of unpleasant names and making it clear she didn't want to see him again. In the circumstances he decided staying away for the night was the best course of action.

He was in his office the following afternoon mulling over whether they could trust Mignemi and if he should feel relieved or concerned that the contract on his life had been removed. He was unable to concentrate on anything and was just killing time until Packham and Mignemi arrived.

Skaa's excitement peaked when he was satisfied he'd entered Kell's number correctly and pressed the green call button on his burner mobile. Kell answered after a couple of rings by simply saying his name and Skaa launched into his pre-prepared diatribe.
'I want you to listen very carefully Mr Kell, because I am the man who is holding the lovely Molly, and if you don't do exactly as I say she will have her pretty little head blown right off. As a sign of good faith, I will be sending you a picture of the young lady which I took the other day when I got her to hold a loaded gun to her head, so you can see that I'm not joking. I don't really care about Molly; although she is quite pretty. What I care about is you Mr Kell, and my lists. So it's important you follow my instructions to the letter. As soon as you receive the picture, I want you to leave your office, go to Liverpool Street and take the Central Line to Leytonstone

where you will wait outside the station for further instructions. If you involve the police then little Molly will become headless. I'm prepared to let her go and you will take her place. Then you are going to endure a slow and agonising death so I can cross you off my list. Goodbye Mr Kell, and please remember that I'm not joking.'

The call ended with near-hysterical laughter, which caused passers-by to give the strange-looking man a wide berth.

He put his phone back in his pocket and pulled out Molly's fancy device that could take pictures. He went through the process she showed him and that he rehearsed maybe fifty times and it went like clockwork.

'See, practice does make perfect,' he said aloud causing more strange looks from people walking by.

He typed the following in the "Add a Caption" box. 'She does take a lovely picture but won't look as pretty without her head. No police or else!' He tapped the blue arrow and the picture and its message disappeared into the ether. He walked a short way down the road and chucked Molly's phone into a waste bin. All he had to do then was wait for Kell to appear.

Kell snapped out of his blank-out by the ding on his phone. He hadn't had an episode when he lost touch with his conscious mind since the boat incident with Andrei Llubov and it took him a few seconds to reconnect with what had just happened. He looked at his phone and saw he had a WhatsApp message. He opened it and saw the photograph of a terrified and dishevelled Molly pointing a gun at her own head. He replayed the one-sided conversation from the phone call and something in the back part of his brain felt like it was lighting up with a crucial piece of information, trying to push through to his full consciousness as a matter of urgency.

I've heard that voice before somewhere; I know I have but where and when, where, and when. He shut his eyes and despite the thoughts of Molly and all the terrible things that had doubtless happened to her and what might happen if he couldn't rescue her, he cleared his mind and let his subconscious seek the answer he was looking for. A minute later he opened his eyes and almost smiled: 'Of course, the would-be client that wasn't happy he refused to take his case!'

Instead of opening up the various files on the office computer, he walked over to the filing cabinet and pulled a folder which was tagged as Not Proceeding, he flicked through the various pieces of paper until he found the one he was looking for.

It had a name, address, and phone number. A Jimmy Skaa who lived in a derelict part of Leytonstone. It was all starting to make sense.

Despite wanting to charge over to free Molly and teach the sick psycho a lesson he would never forget, his police training kicked in. He sat down and thought about the phone call and the message and that he was being lured into enemy territory. How would this Skaa guy know when he got to the Underground station at Leytonstone? There were only two answers. He would either be waiting there for him to arrive, but that could be an indeterminate amount of time. Or did the fact that he'd called him on his landline mean that he was watching him and would, therefore, follow him to the station.

Kell banked on the latter. He locked up the office and headed out hoping to be the hunter and not the hunted.

Kell stood outside his office scrutinising the people scurrying up and down the street who were either heading to their favourite watering hole or going to catch the bus or train that would take them home. He knew his quarry would be watching him but from where?

'Why is he just standing there?' Skaa said aloud. He was on the opposite side of the street in the doorway of a Thai restaurant thirty yards way.

'Because he knows you are out here watching him. Waiting to follow so you know when he gets to the station. You've been rumbled so you need to revert to Plan B.'

'But I haven't got a Plan B. There isn't a list with a Plan B on it.'

'Well, you're going to have to make one and quickly.'

Skaa started to pace up and down outside the restaurant having an animated discussion with himself. It was only the mass of people trooping up and down both sides of the street that kept him from being seen by the man on the other side of the road.

'Calm down you fool. He'll see you and then everything will be lost.'

'What am I going to do? I haven't got a list. This was not supposed to happen!'

'You've only got one option. Go back to the flat, pick up the remaining cash, pack the few belongings that you have, and leave town. You probably have enough time to have some fun with the girl but that would be indulgent and only increase the likelihood that you'll be caught. Now walk away from where he's standing and get to Liverpool Street. You can be back at the flat in forty minutes if you're lucky and then you're on your own.'

'What do you mean "I'll be on my own"?'

'I want nothing more to do with you. You're a loser and a fool. Anyway, you'll probably get caught.

'Fine! I don't need you anyway.' And with that, he set off on a circuitous route back to the station.

Kell's phone rang. He saw it was Packham and declined the call. He didn't need any distractions now. He could find Molly on his own; after all, he now knew for certain that he was responsible. If only he'd taken the crazy man's case.

He decided to widen his search zone. He started to walk up and down both sides of the street covering a distance of forty yards. He reckoned that anything outside this radius would make it unlikely for anyone to see the office door with any clarity. For no reason, he first went east down the road. If he'd chosen to go in the other direction, then everything would almost certainly have turned out different.

Chapter 34

Mignemi decided that it would be safer to meet his team at Stanstead Airport than to have them come to the apartment building. He thought it was unlikely that the Aljadid was still tracking his movements but as the security services operated in such a disparate fashion, he judged it best to be cautious.

He knew the trust he was putting in the young man Hendrick was a risk, but one that he had no choice but to take. His reputation as a bomb maker was without tarnish throughout the Qadim network and his efficiency in Llubovs' escape had been impressive. The big "but" was that he didn't know where his allegiances truly lay. If he was close to Santini and the two had spoken then he fully expected a somewhat different meeting when he arrived at the airport car park.

His other concern was Santini himself. All he could do was hope that he wasn't going to be at the warehouse for any reason. Whilst this was unlikely, it was possible that he'd be on hand if any last-minute concerns relating to the arms shipment cropped up. It wasn't that there was any binding legal document in place; deals like this were agreed by word of mouth and the shake of a hand. But like himself, he was second only to the Maktab itself.

Then if all went as planned, would his friend join him in taking control of the organisation they'd served most of their lives, or would he damn him for the ultimate act of betrayal? He knew these matters were outside of his control, so he put them to the back of his mind as the train pulled into the airport station.

He made his way to the pickup area and started to breathe easier when he saw Hendrick behind the wheel of a modest-looking Hyundai i30. He got in the front passenger seat and the car slowly pulled away.

'Is everything in order?'

'Yes, the explosives are in the false bottom of the suitcase. There is enough to destroy everything within a twenty metre radius. I've briefed Andrei and Darya that they must be at the far end of the corridor when it goes off. This is where the toilets are so you should be safe Alfio. The detonation device is in the glove box.'

Mignemi opened the compartment and took out a modest-looking pay as you go phone.

Hendrick continued: 'I've removed all of the phone workings so there is only the circuitry that links to the bomb. You need to switch the phone on to arm the device. The green button instigates detonation.'

'Is there a time lag from pressing the button to the explosion?' asked Mignemi.

'Less than one second,' replied Hendrick.

'Very good, and you have the other weapons you need?'

He was surprised when it was Andrei who answered. 'Yes, we have multiple options to ensure success. It will be like shooting fish in a barrel.'

'Thank you, Andrei. And Hendrick, what is your plan for the guards?'

'As soon as you go up in the lift, I will stay with the guard in the stairwell, making small talk. At 11:55, I will take him out, no gun just a knife to the heart. He is in radio contact with the two at the car park entrance, but it is not an open channel. It is a standard one way, so they won't be aware of anything untoward. I will then move to take care of the remaining two, again with no noise, using the suppressor on the Glock.'

Mignemi nodded and they completed the rest of the journey in silence.

At precisely 11:40 they entered the underground car park with the two guards just doing a visual check on the four people in the car. Hendrick parked in the spot adjacent to the entrance of the stairwell where the third sentry was waiting. He got the briefcase out the boot and handed it to his boss.

Pleasant greetings were exchanged and the party of three got in the lift and ascended to their date with destiny.

When the lift doors closed, Hendrick switched into full charm mode and started chatting about how terrible the Hyundai was to drive compared to the Audi, but that he knew the sense in keeping a low profile.

When the sentry only grunted a barely intelligible response, he knew instantly that something was wrong. He glanced through the glass in the door to the garage and saw the two front of house guards walking towards the stairwell. Instinct took over and in flash, he pulled the hunting knife from the sheath at the back of his belt and buried into the sentry's stomach. It wasn't a kill strike but gave him enough time to move behind the man desperately trying to stop his intestines leaving his body and snap his neck in one quick movement. He lowered him to the floor and pulled out of the line of sight of the glass in the door. He pulled the Glock and waited for them to step through. Except they didn't. For some reason, they remained in the garage.

It was actually the smart play. Until they had confirmation that the threat had been neutralised they would wait where they could easily take down anyone emerging from the door.

Time was now a critical factor. He hauled the dead man to his feet got him in a bear hug from behind and walked him to the door. Fortunately, it opened outwards into the garage. When there was enough space, they stepped into the open space as one and he pushed the dead man forward. The split second of uncertainty was all he needed. The shock at seeing something that wasn't supposed to happen delayed the guards' response to let him get off two shots as he fell behind the body. Both hit their targets, one looked to be fatal but the other was just a flesh wound in the arm. As he hit the ground, the gun jolted out of his hand and skidded across the garage floor towards the car. The remaining guard had also dropped his gun and both men got their feet at the same time. Hendrick smiled at his opponent as he pulled the hunting knife from its sheath.

The guard stood his ground staring at his opponent. He slowly reached inside his jacket and pulled another gun and slowly raised it returning the smile as he did. The smile turned to a manic grin as Henrick flicked his wrist and sent the knife slicing through the man's chest and into his heart.

He retrieved his weapons and moved the bodies into the stairwell. He knew it was too risky to try to alert his comrades that the double-crossers were being double-crossed themselves. A call or text would almost certainly give them away. His job remained to secure the escape route and trust that they would win the day.

He jogged across the garage to the entrance where the large roller door had been closed. He checked the controls in the booth and opened the door to halfway, estimating the required headroom for the car to get through. When he was satisfied he went back to the Hyundai, turned it around, and waited.

The Aljadid security detail on the corridor was better at concealing any nervousness about the removal of the two men and one woman who came out of the lift. The siblings hung back as agreed and stayed by the lift doors smiling and greeting the five men who stood much closer to the boardroom.

Mignemi walked past them and got to the door which was opened by one of the Al Khamsa personal guards. He walked into the room and immediately sensed the tension in the air.

Irini greeted him with a kiss on both cheeks: 'Welcome Alfio, today is going to be a truly momentous day.' She gestured to the seat he had sat in on his previous visits and he remained standing while he opened the briefcase. He pulled out a number of folders closed the case and put it on the floor beside his chair. It was 11:49.

'These are the details of the Qadim cell structure and their hierarchies of command I have a copy for each of you.' He passed them around and waited until the five had commenced their cursory inspection of the documents.

He knew it was early but his instinct told him something wasn't right.

'I'm sorry, but if you'll excuse me I need to use the bathroom.'

He noticed Irini and Helmut exchange worried glances before Irini said: 'Of course, the end of the corridor on the left by the lifts.' She added: 'You're not thinking of running away are you Alfio?'

Her question had a playful tone, but he knew she was serious.

'Not at all. Providing your people hit the target, the Maktab will very soon be no more.' He smiled and slowly walked to the door.

The boardroom door being opened was not something anyone on the corridor expected. They all clicked into high alert, but nobody produced a weapon.

'Just a bathroom break,' said Mignemi.

The imperceptible nod he gave to the siblings told them the plan had been pulled forward. As he passed them and turned to the door to the washrooms, he said very quietly.

'Now.'

In Beirut harbour, a Sea Spider motor launch moved slowly down the waterfront with six men on board. The boat had been moored in the dockyard area as expected but there was no crew to convince that they would be taking charge of the short ride up the harbour to deliver the deadly cargo. They had checked the weaponry to the manifest. All present and correct. Five hand-held rocket launchers with enough ammunition to blow up the whole harbour if necessary. The man captaining the boat checked the map and the B&G Radar Scanner to confirm their location. He saw the warehouse which stood seventy metres from the quayside which made the overall distance a little shy of two hundred. No problem for the artillery they held. He checked his watch and gave the order to fire. Six deadly missiles streaked towards their target and the warehouse disappeared in a ball of flame. Each man reloaded and a second volley smashed into the crumbling building creating an inferno. The captain turned the boat ninety degrees and headed out to sea.

The huge coast guard ship that was in deep water, docking a hundred metres up the coast watched the events unfold but did not pursue the rogue boat. Instead, the Captain gave an order to his First Officer who picked up a hand-held console and flicked a small metal switch. There was another huge explosion and the rogue boat disappeared in a ball of flames. The spectacle continued for a couple of minutes as the remaining mortars exploded with the heat.

In Holland Park, everything happened at once. The Llubovs produced their semi-automatic Beretta's and started spraying the corridor with bullets. Mignemi pulled the phone/detonator out of his pocket and pressed the green send button. The huge explosion sent him sprawling across the washrooms, he smashed his head into the pedestal of a washbasin and everything went black.

The corridor was filled with smoke and dust. As it cleared Darya saw her brother lying in a pool of blood. In her anger, she sprayed another volley of gunfire down the narrow room before kneeling beside the body and checking for a pulse. He was still breathing. As far as she could see he had been shot in the stomach, not immediately fatal but a wound that needed urgent attention. She left him and went to check that none of the guards would give them any trouble. One was still alive so she put a bullet in his head. Next, she checked the boardroom. Body parts littered the floor. It was hard to tell which part belonged to which body. She counted the heads, five in total, mission accomplished.

She re-entered the corridor and saw a groggy Mignemi stumbling out of the washroom door.

'All dead, mission accomplished but Andrei's been shot. He needs medical attention.'

Together they managed to get him to his feet and she pressed the call button for the lift. She held her breath knowing that if the lift had been blown out of commission then getting her brother down to the car might be one step too far.

The lift door opened, they staggered into the compartment and headed down to the car park.

When his three comrades came into view, all Hendrick could see was a mass of blood. The wound on Mignemi's head was producing a steady stream of dark red fluid and Andrei was bleeding out from his stomach.

Hendrick took control. 'Darya, you drive. Alfio, get in the front and get some pressure on that wound. Put Andrei in the back and I'll see what I can do for him.' He opened the boot and took out a large backpack with "Paramedic" on it and got into the back with the barely conscious Andrei.

'Drive slowly and carefully Darya. Don't do anything to attract attention. I'll do what I can for Andrei and keep your head down Alfio; you look like you've been hit by a tank.'

Hendrick had judged the headroom for the car perfectly and it emerged from the car park without a scratch. In the distance they could hear the sirens of the emergency services but there was no one left to be saved.

Chapter 35

Amy woke with a start and for a split second wondered where she was. The ache in her neck and the sight of the three-quarter empty wine bottle on the coffee table meant she had fallen asleep on the couch waiting for Justin to come home. Clearly, he hadn't.

She was so mad at him when she got his message that "something important had come up" so he wouldn't be able to make the second viewing on the apartment, that she'd lost it and left him a message of a tirade of abuse which culminated in her ending the relationship.

But now in the cold light of day she knew, she'd overreacted. It wasn't like her to be jealous of his work. It was important to him and they both agreed to give each other the space they needed to make a success of their careers. After all, she worked all the hours God sent, so why shouldn't he? She knew in her heart that it wasn't the fact that his working hours were unpredictable, it was that he wouldn't let go of the aftermath of the Horizon Scandal that had nearly gotten both of them killed. He wouldn't let it go, like a dog with a bone. He had to see that justice was served and didn't give a damn about the consequences to their relationship.

When she calmed down, she decided it would be best if she went to see the apartment on her own. Although she got the same warm feeling about the place as on their first visit, she couldn't put in the offer they'd discussed as the resentment of him missing the appointment resurfaced.

By ten o'clock she had started getting concerned that he hadn't come home or called to say why he was late. At this point her stubbornness of not ringing him was at its peak, fuelled by the best part of a bottle of red wine. She must have fallen asleep about eleven and now it was 6:30 and she felt like death warmed up.

She put the kettle on and jumped in the shower with growing anxiety about where he was.

She got to work just after eight, knowing she had back to back meetings until lunchtime. She called his mobile which rang out before going to voicemail and then called his office in case he'd stupidly decided to spend the night there. No reply, straight to the answer machine.

She was about to ring Chris Packham when the boss put his head around her office door; 'Ah good, you're here. Have you got ten minutes for a quick update with the finance guys?'

It was 1:30 before she got a minute to herself and she repeated the process of ringing his mobile and then the office and getting the same result. No reply.

She grabbed her coat and walked into the main office where the executive PAs sat.

'I'm going out for a couple of hours, should be back by four. I'm on my mobile if anyone needs me.'

It took her half an hour to get across town to the east side of the city. She had this strange idea that maybe he was deliberately declining her calls although that would be completely out of character. But in truth, she was now really worried that something had happened to him and the best place to probably find him would be his office.

Just as Packham was leaving his office to get to the Mignemi meeting one of the officers working on the Molly Cribbs disappearance ran up to him almost out of breath.

'Her phone was used earlier this afternoon. A WhatsApp message was sent to a mobile number. We've triangulated the location as the bottom end of Brick Lane. We're just checking the number the message was sent to.'

'No need to do that. It will be Justin Kell, the ex-reporter now private investigator. I'm on my way there now.'

He got out his phone and called up his friend's number from his contacts. It went straight to voicemail.

'Shit! I hope you're not trying to be the knight in shining armour riding out to save the damsel in distress,' he muttered to himself.

'Sir?' enquired the DC.

'Nothing. Look get onto the phone network and see what the message says. Ring me as soon as you've got anything.'

Amy's concerns intensified when she saw a police car parked outside with a man she recognised pressing the intercom and banging on the door.

'Chris? What's going on?'

Packham spun around in surprise: 'Amy, what are you doing here?'

'Justin didn't come home last night and he's not answering his phone. I thought I'd check the office.'

'I can't get hold of him either. Have you got a set of keys for this place? I don't want to have to knock the door down. I'm worried he's had one of his blank-outs and hurt himself.'

Amy rummaged in her bag and brought a key ring with two keys on it and handed it to the policeman.

'The tab on the keyring has the alarm code on it. The panel is on the right as you go to the main office.'

They ran up the stairs, opened the office, and expectantly walked in. Packham switched off the alarm and took it in the room.

'Nothing out of place. The alarm set. He's clearly not here. Christ Justin, where are you?'

Amy gave the policeman a quizzical look. 'Why are you here, Chris? Are the police officially looking for him? Has he done something wrong?'

'Not quite. There's been a development on Molly's disappearance and I think he's trying to sort it himself. Stupid bugger. But we're also due to have a meeting here on another case.'

'Who with?' asked Amy.

And then the intercom buzzed.

Chapter 36

Mignemi's head was slowly clearing as Darya drove them carefully back to Central London. The gash on his head was largely superficial and he'd stopped the bleeding by ruining two of his handkerchiefs.

'We need to get Andrei to a hospital and quickly,' said Hendrick. 'I've slowed the bleeding down but he's lost a lot of blood. He needs a transfusion and antibiotics to avoid infection. There's a bullet in there somewhere as well.'

'If we take him to a hospital he will be arrested for certain,' said Mignemi. 'Is there nothing you can do for him back at the farmhouse?'

'No, I'm afraid not. If we don't get him to a hospital soon, it'll be too late.'

'We must take a chance with the hospital,' said Darya. 'If he dies he's never coming back, at least there's a chance of escape or a deal if he lives.'

Mignemi knew the chance of any deal regarding Andrei Llubov was zero, but it would help his purpose if he could keep him alive and thus deliver him to Packham and his friends.

'Very well. I don't know all the London hospitals but it must be more than just coincidental that we are close to Guys.' He checked Google Maps on his phone and put the directions on the loudspeaker. Just fifteen minutes if the traffic was kind.

'When we get there stop right outside A&E. Hendrick and I will take him in and then leave once we are sure he is being attended to. You can then drop me and Hendrick in the city and you can return to the farmhouse. We will meet you there tomorrow.'

Darya was able to park the car at the entrance to A&E. Hendrick ran in and secured a wheelchair while Mignemi got the wounded man out of the car. His breathing was shallow but he was conscious and Hendrick pushed the wheelchair into the admissions area screaming for help.

A young doctor ran to intercept him asking what had happened.

'He got caught in the crossfire of a gang dispute. I think he's been shot in the stomach,' replied Hendrick.

The doctor took over pushing the wheelchair and said: 'Come with me.'

Hendrick followed for a few steps before turning around and sprinting back to the car. He got in the back seat and Darya drove away.

'A doctor took him straight in and I avoided giving any personal details. I told him he got caught in the crossfire of a gang dispute.'

'Good,' said Mignemi. 'He doesn't have any identification documents on him so they'll be wondering who he is for a while. This may give us an opportunity to get him back.'

'Where about do you want dropping?' asked Darya.

'Anywhere near Aldgate East tube station. Then it's easy for you to carry on down the A11 and head back to Essex. It's best if you don't make any enquiries about Andrei's situation at the hospital. I will get confirmation of his status and we'll take it from there.'

No one spoke as they chugged through the city traffic. Eventually, they reached Whitechapel High Street and the two men got out of the car. As soon as the car pulled away Mignemi turned to the younger man.

'This is a spare access key to my apartment. Go there now and pack all my clothes and personal effects. There are various suitcases in the wardrobe in the main bedroom. I will meet you there as soon as I have attended to some outstanding matters. Later tonight we will fly back to Beirut. You have your passport as I instructed?'

'Yes sir, I have it. But what about Andrei and Darya, are we leaving them behind?'

'The matters that I have to attend to will ensure that both of them are taken care of. There is a much bigger play going on my young friend and you have earned the right to be a part of it. Now please, do as I say.'

Hendrick nodded and hailed a cab as Mignemi headed for Brick Lane and his meeting with the policeman and the investigator.

As he approached Kell's office he was perturbed by the sight of a police car parked outside, it's blue and red warning lights flashing lazily in the afternoon sunshine. He kept to a steady pace walked past the car and buzzed the intercom. His uneasiness grew when he did not get a response. He turned around, looked at the police car, and saw the uniformed man sitting quietly in the driver's seat.

He buzzed again and this time the door clicked open. He walked slowly up the stairs knowing that whatever it was that was wrong; he could do nothing about it.

He opened the door to the office and saw a woman he couldn't immediately name standing next to the policeman. There was no sign of Kell.

Amy turned towards Packham and then back at Mignemi.

'You!' was all her astonishment could manage.

'Ah, of course, Miss Speight. I trust you are keeping well?'

'No, thanks to you and that crazy bitch you set on me.' She moved towards him as if going to slap his face but Packham grabbed her arm and pulled her back.

'Amy, this has nothing to do with you. I have an important meeting with Mr Mignemi so can you please go and wait in the police car outside.'

She wasn't going anywhere. 'Why are you meeting here in Justin's office and not at the police station?'

Packham sighed and sat down in one of the chairs by the meeting table.

'Justin should be here as well. It was at his request.' He pointed at Mignemi noticing the gash on his head.

'I wanted to let your friend know that the threat to his life has been removed. Mr Packham, I assume you've been able to secure the other terms I asked for?'

'Amy, please go and wait in the car. I just need five minutes with Alfio and then we can get back to finding Justin.'

'I'm not going anywhere. Consider me Justin's representative.' She sat down opposite the policeman with a defiant stare fixed on her face.

Mignemi remained standing. 'So, Mr Kell is missing? Well, let me assure you that it has nothing to do with me. Now Mr Packham, if you have secured my terms then I will give you the information I promised.'

'Yes, all your terms will be met, so start talking.'

He paused, gathering himself as if the reality of the last few hours had only just struck home.

'Just before midday, there was an explosion at a private members club in Holland Park. The club is a front for the headquarters of the Aljadid. The five members of their high command died in the explosion. This I verified with my own eyes. Their security detail which also numbered five were also killed. Three guards in the garage area below the building also died, but not in the explosion. I know you are aware of the office in the Shard which they use with a brass plate called Wirebound Electronics as the front. They also use a restaurant in Soho called the Bistro.' He took a card he'd picked up from one of his visits out of his wallet and flicked it across the table towards the policeman.

'A man known as Alex appears to run various operations out of this restaurant. They are rudderless Mr Packham, so strike now and you will rid London of this scum once and for all.'

'And what of the Maktab? Were they also taken care of?' asked Packham.

'Events at Holland Park did not go quite as planned so I cannot verify their destruction at this time. When I return to Beirut later today I will know for certain, and I will contact you to confirm. If everything has proceeded as planned, then I will cease all Qadim operations in London.'

'Very well, and what of the Llubovs?'

'Andrei was wounded in the stomach. He is at Guy's hospital. He has no ID so the doctors don't know who he is. They believe he got caught up in some local gang warfare.'

He turned towards Amy. 'Darya has returned to a farmhouse in Thaxted, close to Stanstead Airport.' He scribbled the address on a pad that was lying on the table.

'There are approximately six Qadim operatives there. They are all armed so I would approach with caution.' He paused. 'Now that is all that I have. There is a British Airways flight to Beirut this evening and I trust you have my ticket?'

Packham pulled the airline ticket out of his pocket and pushed it across the table.

'A one-way ticket, Alfio. I never want to see you again.'

Mignemi stood up. 'Goodbye Miss Speight, I hope you find your friend soon.' He turned and left the office as Packham started to make a number of frantic phone calls.

Amy was stunned by what she had heard. She was amazed that Justin was so deeply involved in such extreme police business and close to tears as she realised how much he had kept from her.

Packham had finished barking out the various instructions to act on the information received and looked at Amy wondering what he could say. He opened his mouth to begin when his phone rang. He listened intently and ended the call.

'We've got a trace on Justin's phone. We know where he is. Come on.'

They raced down the stairs, jumped into the police car, hoping that they wouldn't be too late.

Chapter 37

Kell did one loop up and down the line of sight of his office. When he didn't see anyone acting suspiciously he started to sprint down Fournier Street towards the station. If he was correct that the strange Mr Skaa had taken Molly as a bizarre tit for tat for him not taking his case, then it was a straight race to get to his flat in Leytonstone ahead of him.

He barrelled down the side of Spitalfields Market pushing people out of his way. He ran straight across Bishopsgate narrowly avoiding a bus and into the station. He used his debit card to tap through the barrier and charged down the steps to the Central Line. He pushed to the edge of the platform glaring at anyone who rebuked him, muttering that it was an emergency and forced himself onto the already overcrowded train.

He was breathing hard as the tube pulled away. Just five stops to Leytonstone. Five stops to Molly. He shut his eyes and said a prayer hoping he was ahead of the lunatic. If he got there first he knew he could save her.

Skaa also had a frantic urgency to get back to his flat as quickly as possible. He was unsure what Kell actually knew, but he wasn't going to abandon his plan at the first sign of trouble. He rushed back to the station as fast as he could, his confidence growing that he was still in control.

Now that he was on the tube, Kell waited for his heart rate to slow down and tried to picture how things were unfolding. He rationalised that it was likely that he was leading the race, and that once he got to the property he'd have at least ten minutes to free Molly if she was still alive. Once she was safe he'd call Packham and let the police take over. If he came across Skaa, then he'd deal with him, full stop.

He ran up the stairs at Leytonstone underground and tapped out with his debit card. He was pretty sure he knew how to get to 7A Ringmore Street but needed to make certain he didn't get lost or take any wrong turns. He opened up Google Maps, typed in the address, and started following the instructions. He walked as quickly as he could and no more than five minutes later, stood outside an end terrace house on a run-down street, which didn't exactly look like anyone was living in it. The number 7A was screwed near the top of the door on a faded brass plate.

He didn't hesitate. He slammed the sole of his foot into the door and what must have been a weak lock gave in easily with some of the door frame. He stepped inside and felt for a light switch behind the door. He flicked it on and took in a room that resembled a bomb site. There was a filthy looking settee covered in empty food cartons and various cans of soft drinks. It was stained and dirty with damp patches all over it. There was a small coffee table with more empty cartons and numerous black books that looked like diaries. Paper was strewn everywhere. He scanned the room and saw a door in the back left-hand corner next to a filthy sink full of dirty dishes and mugs. Something caught his attention. A noise maybe. He stood still and listened, straining his ears.

Molly was dozing when she heard a loud bang from upstairs. She stirred from her exhausted slumber and for the first time in days she felt a glimmer of hope. She started screaming.

Kell ran across the room, pulled open the door to the cellar, and went carefully down the steps. He could hear Molly shouting and screaming but the room was dark and he couldn't see her. He flicked on the light on his mobile and scanned the desolate scene.

'Justin, thank God you came.' Molly screams turned to tears as she stood up and waited for her hero to free her.

Kell ignored the terrible smell of the dank cellar as he held Molly in his arms. When they eventually broke the embrace she looked into his eyes and kissed him full on the lips. He briefly kissed her back.

'Is there a light in this hell hole?' he asked.

'Yes at the top of the stairs,' she replied.

Kell quickly found the light switch and took in the full desolation of the dungeon.

'What's that in the corner?'

'That's Gary Jones. The mad man shot him.'

'Who is he? It doesn't make sense that he'd do all this just because we wouldn't take his case.'

'He knows you from when you were a policeman. Some job you were on. He blames you for getting him sent to prison. Gary said his real name is Dodds. He met him in prison and they had a bit of trouble. I think he's trying to take revenge on all the people who've wronged him.'

Kell nodded. 'I remember Dodds alright. He was a bent copper involved with a people-trafficking ring. I was undercover at the time, but it must have been seven or eight years ago.'

'He's completely mad Justin; we've got to get out of here before he comes back.'

'Okay, do you know where he keeps the keys to these locks?'

Neither of them had noticed the scar-faced man slowly coming down the steps. He stopped at the bottom and raised the gun he was holding in his right hand.

It was the snigger that made them turn around.

'I've got the keys here Justin,' he held them in his left hand and gave them a shake.

'Now luckily for you, there's room for one more down here since dear old Gary checked out. Now go across to those chains over there and clip them onto your ankles. That'll do for a start. Then we can work on making you a bit more comfortable.'

Kell didn't move, he just stared at the man holding the gun, taking in the madness in his eyes and assessing how likely he was to shoot him. He knew if he put on the shackles that it would certainly end badly for him and Molly and that was something that he just couldn't let happen.

'You said you would let Molly go if I came here. So once you've set her free, I'll get in the shackles. You are going to keep your word, aren't you?'

Skaa looked like he was processing what Kell had said as though it involved a huge logical effort. He hoped the *Voice* would help him out but there was nothing there.

Eventually, he said: 'I will, just as soon as you've secured yourself. I'll let the lovely Molly go. But not before I've taken care of you. I want her to witness you begging for mercy as I cut up your face and remove your eyes. Now move!'

The police car sped away with Packham barking instructions to the driver.

'What's happened, Chris? Is Justin all right? Do you know where he is?'

'He used his debit card to enter the underground at Liverpool Street and then at Leytonstone to exit the station. This was shortly after I left him. He then used Google Maps which took him to an address close to the station. That was the last signal we got from his phone.'

'How long till we get there?'

'Twenty-one minutes,' the driver answered.

'Haven't we met before somewhere?' asked Kell. 'You're face is familiar.' He started to edge towards the psycho as he spoke.

'I've been following you all over London,' Skaa replied proudly. 'Your favourite curry house on Monument Street, the restaurant in Holborn where you had lunch with your pretty girlfriend. I even stood next to you when you were paying for your coffee in that breakfast place where you met the old man. Oh, I know all about you mister big shot investigator, but you know nothing about me.'

'I know you were a bent copper who I helped put away for smuggling innocent women and children. I know your real name is Dodds and not the ludicrously made up Skaa and I know that the police will be here in a couple of minutes to take you away and bang you up for the rest of your miserable life. That's what I know.' He kept his voice calm and considered and edged a little closer to the wrong end of the gun.

Skaa was visibly taken aback by the verbal assault and was struggling to process the information he'd heard. Finally, the *Voice* reappeared in his head.

'He knows who you are, he knows what you were and the police are moments away. If I were you I'd kill them both and get out of here now. You can always start again somewhere else.'

'Yes, yes, good idea. I'll do that.'

Kell sensed the man was about to explode and moved his position slightly to his left to put himself as far away from Molly as he could.

Skaa smiled as he retook his aim.

The armed response unit and ambulances arrived at 7A Ringmore Street at the same time as Packham.

'Stay in the car Amy, let's hope we're in time.' He got out and spoke to the Unit commander.

'You have to go straight in. We believe there are two civilians being kept hostage both hopefully still alive. One male one female. Have you got the footprint of the building from the council?'

'Yes, just the one room at ground level and a cellar. We'll proceed to the basement that's most likely where they're being held.'

Packham nodded. The Commander turned away and gave the instruction to enter the building. 'Set with a single shot. Two hostages male and female. Target likely to be armed. Single file entry on the QT, targets presumed to be in the cellar. Go!'

Skaa hadn't bothered to close the door when he'd got back to the flat. The lock was broken in any case. The two armed officers entered the flat and scoped out the main room. Nothing.

The door to the cellar was open and the sound of voices could just be made out.

'Now let me think about this? What would be for the best? If I just shot you it would be a bit of an anti-climax. You'd just die and wouldn't suffer very much at all. Whereas if I shot Molly then that would hurt, wouldn't it? If only for a couple of seconds before I killed you.'

He turned the gun towards Molly, pulled the trigger and the room exploded with the sound of gunshots.

Skaa sank to the floor with a look of bewilderment on his face. He felt the back on his neck which was a sticky mass of blood and bone. He keeled over onto his side. Dead.

The two shots had been virtually simultaneous. Kell ran to Molly who was unconscious on the floor bleeding from her chest. He ripped off her blouse and saw that the bullet had shattered a couple of ribs but hopefully missed any major organs. Officer number two shouted the all clear and the cellar filled with paramedics, followed by the Unit Commander and Packham.

'The keys to the manacles are there on the floor,' said Kell pointing to where the now dead man had dropped them. Officer number one unlocked the gruesome chains whilst the paramedic tended to Molly focusing on stopping the bleeding.

'It doesn't look like any serious damage has been done. Let's get her into the ambulance quickly.'

'I'll carry her,' said Kell. He gathered her in his arms, carried her up the stairs, and out into the fresh air.

He laid her on the waiting gurney, bent over and gently kissed her on the lips. The paramedics whisked her into the ambulance and sped off with sirens wailing.

Amy watched from the back of the police car with tears slowly trickling down her cheeks.

Chapter 38

Mignemi got back to his apartment forty-five minutes later. Hendrick had dutifully packed up his clothes into two medium-sized suitcases and was casually watching daytime television when Mignemi walked through the door.

'Thank you, Hendrick. There is a BA flight to Lebanon this evening at nine o'clock. Book yourself a ticket and make your own way to the airport. I will be on the flight too, but I suggest we travel separately. When we land I will brief you on the aftermath of successfully taking down the Aljadid leadership and the next steps in the operation.'

'Sure,' said Henrick as he started to tap on his smartphone to book the plane ticket.

'I suggest you get yourself some hand luggage otherwise it will look suspicious. There is a suitable holdall in the spare room.'

'Thanks, I'll pick up a change of clothes before heading to the airport. Is everything okay? What are we going to do about Darya and the other guys at the farmhouse?'

'I need to finalise various matters before I leave. I'll give you a full update in Beirut later tonight. Now, if you'll excuse me I have lots to do.'

Hendrick took that as his cue to leave and headed for the door.

'Oh and Hendrick, one more thing. Thank you for your service and loyalty. I will make sure you are appropriately rewarded.'

The young man nodded and left the apartment.

Mignemi sank onto the settee that Hendrick had just vacated. A great sense of relief oozed out of him. So far, so good. No significant setbacks and just one phone call to make. He picked up his phone and called Santini.

The plane took off on time and the flight was uneventful. Four hours thirty minutes later, they touched down at Rafic Hariri and Mignemi waited in his seat until the rest of the passengers had disembarked. He walked purposefully down the walkway towards passport control. He could see Hendrick ahead of him about to present himself to the official but doubted there would be an issue with a native returning home.

When it was his turn, the man in the booth simply scanned his passport and said, 'welcome back to Beirut Mr Mignemi, I hope you have a pleasant stay.'

Hendrick was waiting by the carousel and dutifully pulled off the two suitcases when they appeared. He loaded them onto a trolley and they headed out of the exit. Amongst the numerous drivers with their small placards showing the name of their passenger, was one which said MIGNEMI.

They followed him out to the short stay car park and the driver loaded the suitcases into the boot of a C Class Mercedes.

'Mr Santini apologises for not being here to greet you himself, but he would like to meet with you now despite the lateness of the hour.'

They drove for thirty minutes through quiet streets into the business district. They stopped outside an office block and a concierge opened the car doors and helped them out.

The driver stayed in the car and advised them he would take their luggage to the Sheraton Hotel, where rooms had been booked for them.

'Mr Santini seems to have taken care of everything,' said Hendrick as they followed the concierge to the lifts.

Mignemi paused and looked at the young man as he let him walk ahead into the lift. The concierge joined them and pressed the button for the nineteenth floor.

When the lift door opened Santini was there to greet them.

He hugged Mignemi and kissed both his cheeks. He repeated the act with Hendrick.

'Come, my office is this way.'

He led them down the corridor and opened a set of double doors halfway down on the left. He stood back to let his guests go first with Mignemi leading the way.

Mignemi entered the room and stopped dead in his tracks.

Sitting around a semi-circular table where the remaining seven members of the Maktab.

Once Santini and Hendrick were in the room and the door closed, it was the eldest sitting in the centre who spoke.

'Welcome Alfio. Please step forward so we can all see you properly.'

He shuffled forward in a daze. How could these people still be alive?

'You seem surprised to see us Alfio? We might be old, but we are not stupid. Did you really think we'd be anywhere near a warehouse on the docks when we are finalising an arms shipment?'

Mignemi stood stock still saying nothing.

'You had done so well up until then. We were very much looking forward to you taking your seat with us.' He gestured to the left end of the semi-circle where there as a vacant chair.

'You did everything to the letter. You gained the trust of the Aljadid leaders and successfully destroyed them. But then you got greedy and forgot your loyalties.' He nodded to Santini.

'I intentionally let it slip that the date of the meeting of our leaders had changed and that was why I had to fly back here. We wanted to see what you would do. The final test you could say.'

The elder continued: 'A test that you failed. You got greedy. Greedy for power and control.'

Santini picked up the lecture: 'And then you betrayed your comrades and made a pathetic deal with the London policeman. You gave up Andrei, who got injured when fighting for you and gave up our base near the airport in Stanstead.'

Mignemi finally spoke: 'But how do you know?'

'You should be more careful who you trust,' said Hendrick.

Santini continued: 'If only you'd showed the same loyalty, my old friend. Thanks to Hendrick here we were able to salvage something from your treachery.'

Mignemi turned as the doors behind him opened and Darya Llubov walked into the room.

'Hendrick warned me not to go to the farmhouse. I couldn't save my brother from going to prison, but I can save your soul Alfio.' She pulled a gun with a long suppressor and shot Alfio Mignemi twice in the head.

Epilogue

Packham and Kell sat at their usual table in their favourite Indian restaurant, sipping lager whilst waiting for their food to be delivered.

It was a week since the dramatic events in Leytonstone and Packham had been busy writing up his reports as well as following up on Mignemi's intelligence.

'So Andrei Llubov is finally back in prison. That's a result,' said Kell.

'Sure was. It was strange. He just confessed to the Henry Gray murder and spilled all he knew about their escape and the assassinations in Holland Park. It was as though he was seeking redemption, trying to purge his soul of all the wrongs he had ever done. He knows he's been betrayed by Mignemi and I think he hopes what he tells us will help us to put him away too.'

'And will it?' asked Kell.

'Unlikely. I'm not bound by any promises we made him. It was a fair exchange. He gave us the Aljadid and the Llubovs. Well one of them anyway and we let him leave the country. What Llubov has told us means we could arrest him if he ever turned up back here? But I'm more interested in hearing if what he said about the Maktab being taken out is true. And if they really have finished their filthy trade here in London.'

'Where is the sister?'

'Well, she wasn't at the farmhouse. It was certainly a Qadim safehouse and we picked up half a dozen minions, but they just keep saying they're farmhands on a non-working farm! It wouldn't surprise me if she slipped out of the country somehow.'

'You're the local hero then. What are the chances of a promotion?' asked Kell.

'Very good apparently. I've been recommended to go before the evaluation board but any DCI job will mean moving out of London. Funnily enough, there's a position up in your old neck of the woods in Manchester. I've had it on the QT that it's mine if I want it.'

'You don't sound too convinced?'

'I'm a London boy, Justin. I've lived and worked here all my life. I'm not sure I could move all that way.'

'All that way! It's only a couple of hours on the train. You should go for it. I mean it. A few years up there and you could come back.'

'You're probably right, but how will you manage without me?'

Kell didn't reply and took a long drag on his drink.

Packham waited for his friend to put his glass down. 'How is Amy? Are you sorting things out?'

'Not really. She keeps saying I lied to her about my involvement in the Mignemi case, but as you know, I really didn't do anything. She says she can't trust me not to go and get myself killed.' He paused finished his drink and gestured to the waiter for two more.

'It's more than that though. It's the Molly thing. She thinks we're involved or going to get that way. Despite what I say, she struggles with the fact that when she gets out of hospital we'll be back working together.'

'Do you have feelings for Molly? And remember, I'm a policeman, so don't lie to me.'

Kell laughed. 'There's definitely something there, some chemistry. She's back at work in a couple of weeks and I must say I'm looking forward to it.'

Their starters arrived and the conversation paused as they tucked into the food.

When they finished the meal, Packham paid the bill and they headed out into the late evening sunshine.

'So what are you going to do?' asked Packham.

Kell shook his head. 'I don't know. I really don't know.'

The End